Author:

Lisa Nicol

Cover Illustration:

Dulce Dorado

Lisa Nicol Sanchez

Book Illustrations:

Dulce Dorado

Lisa Nicol Sanchez

Context Editing:

Lisa Nicol Sanchez

©2010

BREW

Lisa Nicol

ISBN 978-0-359-19900-6

Acknowledgments

I would like to thank everyone and my family without whose help this book would never have been completed.

Thank you for your patience and guidance, to everyone who has been patient with me throughout the 9 years it has taken to finish this book due to my procrastination and hesitation.

Chapter

1

Bye-Bye Little

Little Falls, MN. A place I grew up in and loved deeply, but now a place I hated. I didn't want to lose my mother; what child wants to lose the woman that gave them birth and life and everything they could have ever wanted and desired in this world, I sure didn't - and I became mad at the world, angry at myself—was it me, I questioned; like I had brought the sickness to her body.

Why do I have to lose everyone I love and care for, I just didn't understand.

These past few months have been a swirl-wind of emotions, and a girl can only try to keep it together. Just last year, I lost my father. He was killed trying to escape from a burning building; he was a firefighter and one of the best that Little Falls could have had. When he passed away, another part of my heart broke off. He was the second of my close-knit family to have had an untimely death. My world feels like it is falling apart, and I am unsure of where I will go now. I have no other family here in Little Falls; neither one of my parents' families was that big.

This is what scared me the most; I'm only 15 and don't want to go into foster care. Kids in foster care are looked down on, like dirt...like a lost puppy that nobody wants, that they feel sorry for, and a mandatory chore instead of a wanted child.

I'll be turning 16 this year, and I'm a sophomore at Columbia High School, the school full of pep, full of life, and at this moment all I feel his pain, hurt, dishonesty, and despair. I walked around the halls at school as if I had seen a ghost, not wanting to talk to anybody because they would ask - they would ask what was wrong with me, for those who didn't know and I just wasn't prepared to answer the dark question that haunts me. My grades were declining dramatically; I felt numb; I want to run in a hole and die if I died at least I'd be with my family.

What I am going through is not something a 15-year-old girl needs to go through nor think or feel. I should be worrying about homecoming and football games, but all I'm wondering about is how I'm going to arrange the flowers on my mother's grave.

But bad news travels fast in this little town and even quicker in a nosey prep high school. Everyone around me knew about my mother's death. Every time I was near someone, they would try to get answers out of me.....to find out what happened and to see how I was feeling, but the truth was - I really don't want to talk to anyone. I could barely get through the night without crying myself to sleep. Just hearing her name gets me choked up and teary-eyed. I just rather avoid the whole conversation and pretend like it didn't happen. Pretend, like she is on vacation and will just walk through the doors, pretend ...pretend, it's such a foreign word, to use that word would be deception in my delirious mind. Pretend.....

March 6 was my mother's funeral; it was a complicated process, in which; I wished I didn't have to plan, but it had to be done. Rare purple roses, with white lining, shining bright like amethyst crystals in a sweet spring afternoon; lay on top of her burgundy-colored coffin, beautifully etched design scanned the top. I knew my mother would be proud that I could handle this so delicately and flawlessly; after all, I am only a teenager.

During the ceremony, my mind wandered, and I kept daydreaming, what my life will now be like, and how my future will change. I kept thinking about my new home and new life. Each one of my parents had only one sibling. My mother had one sister, who I had never met, and my father had one kid brother, my crazy Uncle Mike; who is not capable of taking care of a dog, let alone a teenage girl? He is always traveling out of the country. He is an international accountant, whatever that means; he's a typical, young single guy, James Bond slicked back hair with speckled hazel eyes; a man who was proud to be a self-proclaimed bachelor and didn't want that to change. He was in town for a while, just until the will-reading was over, and then I would see where I would now call home.

The following day was my mother's will reading.... both excited and scared

I guess this is where I find out; where I would go.

I held my breath while images of my mother danced through my head, and until my cheeks turned purple, so nervous at that moment, I forgot how to breathe - as her lawyer read the will.

He explained that my mother left all her assets to me as I am her only living child; it was natural. The next one blew me away......

She wanted me to go live with her sister—Gertrude ... in Salem, Massachusetts!

"What!" I exclaimed as those words rolled out of his chapped lips.

"I can't," as I pouted like a little girl baby.

I couldn't believe this—What I feared more than the worst. I did not know who this lady was, and she lived thousands of miles away from my home, my wonderful home, my beautiful home, at least if I were put into foster care, I could stay here in Little Falls

and still be with my friends. I got angry at the fact that my

mother would do this. I felt betrayed, hurt, a whole range of

emotions went through my body. She knew how important my

friends are, and she took my last hope of a semi-happy life away.

"Got your wish?" I rudely muttered to my uncle Mike. He had

come into town and was almost just as much as a nervous wreck

like me. As I shoved my chair back into the dusted warped wall,

that I was sluggishly sitting in front of, storming

out of the room, racing down the hallway, the walls seemed to

close in on me, and my crumbling life went flying out the front

doors of the lawyer's building. Falling onto the cracked front

steps, I threw my head in my hands and sobbed.

"Not again!" was all I could think of while slamming my fist into

the ground.

A hand touches mine; I gazed up with tears in my sad-stricken

eyes; it was my Uncle Mike.

"Are you okay?" he politely said to my grieved mind.

"No…. no, I'm not!" I cold-heartedly stared at him, as if it was his fault that my mother is sending me away, "You got what you wanted!".

My uncle Mike was surprised but happy that he didn't have to give up his bachelor lifestyle to care for a teenage girl.

I have no other choice but to have fun while I can, and so the countdown begins. March 31, I would leave for Salem; I guess I can fuss and cry all I wanted, but I have to go, pick myself up, wipe the tears from my cold cheeks and deal with the disappointment, so I guess I will make the best out of this while it lasts.

Tomorrow, my best friends will throw me a "going away" party. I appreciated them for all they have done for me. They know this isn't what I want, but they are respectful of my mother's decisions if only I could feel the same way.

Arriving back home, I ran up the front stairs to our old Victorian-style house, laced with brick. I get inside, and a burst of sorrow hits me like a wrecking ball against a cement building.

I left my Uncle Mike back in the car, to bring himself in. I wanted to take a few minutes by myself. I'm glad I get to stay at my house for at least the next few weeks. I acknowledged sometimes I had taken for granted, but just feeling the love that grew in this house over the past years; I got chills; I shook and felt weak. I couldn't breathe…As I walked down the hallway…. Passing my hands along the pale, pigeon grey walls, nicely decorated with photos of us as a united family. It crumbles my heart into pieces, just thinking of having to leave it. I wish I could take part of this with me.

 Reaching the end of the hallway, I get to my parents' room; I had not opened this door since before my mother passed.

"Dare I open it," I pressed my mind in questionable doubt.

I reached for the brass-colored knob, that was beautifully connected to the cherry wood door, that connected my past to my future. I slowly started to turn the knob; my heart was sinking, my stomach bubbling…… I pulled myself back and retraced my wandering thoughts.

I quickly turned around and ran up the stairs as my uncle Mike made his way inside.

"Sands…" He calls. I turn, and we lock eyes; he knew I didn't care to talk; he knew there was nothing he could say right now. I continued my way up the grieved stricken staircase and got to my room. Locking my door, throwing my headphones on, and *I tried to* relax my mind. Happy thoughts, Sandy... Happy thoughts.

Chapter

2

Prepare

The following day was my party; I was so touched and felt loved; we gushed and cried and shared old pictures of us throughout the years.

"I wish you didn't have to go," Julie cried. Julie was the funny one, always making me smile, her Auburn loose curly hair and green eyes made her an even more of a beautiful person.

"I will miss you all so much," I choked, "you girls are my sisters, I don't know how I will manage," I began to get teary all over again.

"The four musketeers in the same room for the last time," Fayth cried aloud as we all began to hug one another.

The thought of leaving them so saddened me; my heart broke once more, losing the only other "family" I had. We were not blood, but they have been in my life since we were babies, and they are my sisters, regardless.

Everyone brought me presents, and we took more pictures as we were unsure if this would be our last time seeing each other - forever.

My long time "guy-friend," KY Doyle, was also there. He greeted me with a warm kiss on the cheek and a pretty wrapped present.

With his calm, sensual voice, he says, "Open it, Sandy, I hope you like it," He stared at me with his bright blue eyes and dirty blonde hair.

I opened this big red box, and inside of the big box was a smaller box, and inside the smaller box was a tiny turquoise box wrapped with a white ribbon. I felt like I was playing with a Russian doll. "Geez, KY, what's with all the boxes?" I chuckled, thinking this was a joke.

Opening the last box, I could not believe my eyes. It was beautiful….just sitting there was a gold ring with two little hearts that intertwined with each other!

My eyes dart upwards, him with a thumb on his top lip, while he stares at me, waiting for a reply.

"Wow! KY, this ring is beautiful," the words left my lips, "so sweet and thoughtful of you, but I can't take this," I admitted to him nervously.

"Sure you can, Sands," he said with reassurance. He reaches for my hand to grab the box.

"Hold on to it," he says as he takes the ring from the box, "because I will never let my love for you go and when you are ready, put it on, then I will know that you want me too," he sets it in my palm and kisses my hand.

Kindly smiling back at him, "Okay," was the only response I could let out without sounding too 'eager.'

I mean, I have feelings for KY, but I don't want to lose our friendship. You can tell the love between the two of us, and everyone knows we have deep feelings of passion but to keep me from being hurt; I instead love him secretly than to lose him forever.

After KY's surprising gift, Julie, Fayth, and Alex said they had a huge present for me. I was so nervous; I have no clue what these girls could have gotten me. They are always full of surprises, even though I'm not fond of surprises, I'll take theirs any day.

"Close your eyes!" Julie hyper-ly squills...

Impatiently waiting for what seemed to be a lifetime, they scream, "Okay, you can look now."

I opened my eager eyes to an envelope.

I thought in my head, "That's it?"

Alex, the hyper one of us four, jumped up and down, "Open it, open it!" looking like a spider monkey clinging to my arm to a point it turned purple.

I wasted no time and ripped through the blue envelope tied with a gold bow. It was miles - for a round-trip plane ticket back to Little Falls, so I could come back and visit.

"You know my dad travels a lot and is more than happy to give you his flyer miles," Julie informed me.

My eyes filled up with tears.

"I will miss you, girls," I cried to them as we group hugged.

Flashbacks of our childhood ran through my mind like a

marathon, and I thought about everything we have been through so much in the ten years we have known each other. I don't know how I will cope in Salem without them.

The next day was a complete opposite of the beautiful farewell party that my besties threw for me. I felt sad and miserable; I didn't want to move to Salem. I know I sound like I'm whining and well….. I AM! I think this is all a dream that is recurring and has no end; I wanted to scream, "WAKE UP SANDY, WAKE UP!" but this nightmare doesn't seem to an end.

Today in school was horrible. The "pretty girls" as we call them comprised Danijela, Tabby, Lucy, and Giselle, they were calling me a witch; this was extremely confusing and just as annoying! Unlike others in this school, I wasn't afraid to confront these girls, I went to them with a straight face, and my head held high, and my hands in a fist wanted to punch them right in their perfectly chiseled faces.

"What's your problem?" saying this to Danijela's back as she turns around, almost smacking me in the face with her long dried out, dyed blonde locks.

"Um," she lets out of her Barbie pink lipstick covered mouth, "You.."

"If you must bug me," She begins.

I roll my eyes, "What's your problem, what is with the witch bull…..?".

"You're moving to the heart of where the Salem Witch Trials were held," she annoyingly sighed as I stared at her crusty eyelashes in confusion.

"I guess you are dumber than you look," Giselle said from Danijela's left side and smirking like a little snake pet of Danijelas.

"You would know?" I tilt my head to mock their cockiness. She rolls her pale eyes

"Let's go, girl, before her stupidity rubs off on us," Danijela demanded to the rest of her 'pack,'

Flipping her long hair back, she turned around, and the *Barbie*

pack followed, walking away with their noses stuck up–any

higher and they could predict the weather.

   As I tried to hold myself back from running after her and

pulling her hair out of her head, I thought, and I remember

hearing about those stories; I don't believe in silly stories like

that. I mean come on.... witches!? Please - the only witch around

is that scary, old lady, Mrs. Rocker down the street, she has like

20 cats!

As if having 20 cats makes you a witch.

Aside from the troubles at school today, KY wants to come over

to my house; he wants to talk about the *'ring.'* I didn't think there

was anything to talk about, but he was so persistent, I agreed.

   When KY arrived later that day, I stood there watching out of

our big garden window that faced the world. He looked so good,

and always dressed nicely to the *'T,'* Khaki pants that fit just

right, and a black polo, that seemed to be painted on his body.

His dirty blonde hair, which had a tint of auburn to it when hit by the sunlight, most perfectly, something I was attracted to, and he knew it.

I removed myself from the window before he noticed me gawking over his gorgeous facial features and rushed to the door, nearly tripping over my own two feet. Before he could even fix his hand to knock on the door, I swung it open…. surprising him, He laughs, "Hey Sands," As he steps through the front door, "What've you been up to?" He asked as if he knew I was stalking him from my bay window.

"Not much," was my response as I led him to my living room, with a sense of calmness.

I closed my eyes for a second, smelling the scent of his cologne, which seemed to surround me from behind as I get lost in his scent. I kept my eyes closed for too long, tripping over the area rug as we arrived in the living room.

"I'm just so clumsy today," I chuckle embarrassed. Turning around, I notice him watching me closely, with a half-smile.

Sitting down on the couch, with him next to my side, he reaches

for my face and kisses me with such passion; I was surprised at

the emotion and was not expecting it. His lips were so soft and

warm. I wanted to linger there a little longer, but I knew I

couldn't expose my true feelings towards him. I pushed KY back,

biting my lip in the aftermath and turning away, I had to stop him

from getting too heavy. As I pushed him again, he grabbed my

left thigh with his right hand.

"KY," I sternly said as I stood up, "I don't want our friendship to

get destroyed."

"It won't......," as he stood up to match my assertiveness while

trying to grab my waist and pulling me closer, to kiss me again.

"KY, I am moving out of town, and we cannot be together,"

backing away from him, I responded to his pushy sexual desires.

"Sandy, I'll follow you to Salem... I will follow you anywhere,"

he stares at me, "until the dawn breaks and the earth stops

moving," his tongue lightly licks his bottom lip.

I laughed as he pulled me towards him, "Nothing will stop me from being with you... I promise!" he assured himself.

"You don't understand KY….. I JUST want a friendship…..," His eyes seem to sadden.

"That is most important right now between the two of us, and I hope you can understand that," I responded to him while sitting back down, "I need a ... friend."

"I don't care," as he pushed his promise and went for yet another embracing encounter while placing his hand on mine.

"Well, I do," as I removed my hand from under his extremely hot palms.

With eyes like the devil, red and weary, the sound of those words was like nails on a chalkboard to his ears.

"Fine, Sandy…. your wish is my command," as he sarcastically stood up and bowed while growing angry, storming out of my living room, out the front door, slamming it so hard he broke the glass vase by the front door. He seemed to run towards his car like someone was chasing him. Hopping in the right after giving me one more look that sent shivers down my spine, he drove off like a madman knocking over the neighbor's trash cans and scaring Mrs. Rocker's cats from sight.

I cannot believe he was acting like a child, and I didn't like it–not one bit. He is just getting a little obsessed with me; it is scaring me. Not only was he changing as he was approaching his 18th birthday physically but mentally. I really don't want this kind of drama, especially weeks after the death of my mother. I hope he will understand and respect my wishes and put this to rest; I don't want to lose him as a friend either.

After that day with KY, everything went fabulous; my *girls* and I went shopping. I needed a little splurging time after the ordeal with KY. I didn't want to tell them too much, or even that KY had kissed me! But you know how it is when girls get together and so it began.

As we ate, at the food court, I told the girls detailed events of the encounter last night, and I only told them things I thought mattered.

As I was explaining the nightly rendezvous, their faces were filled with smirks and smeyes.

"So, he kissed you!" Alex gawked and giggled.

"Yes, please don't repeat that," They all laughed and giggled.

"KY is changing a lot, and it's scaring me," I complained, "It is making me feel uncomfortable to be around him!" I filled the girls in on my thoughts, knowing they thought KY and I could be an item.

"Don't worry, Sands- he is just sad and depressed because you're moving somewhere so far away–you know he wants you," Julie says as she sips on her milkshake with a smirk on her face and eyebrows to the sky.

"That still does not give him an excuse to act like a jerk with me," I replied with force towards her, as I dipped my fries in the overly poured mustard packets. My mind is so messed up right now because YES, I have feelings for KY, and NO, I can't be with him, too much, too soon.

While the girls chatted, my mind just wandered in and out and maybe, just maybe.... KY and I.

As we finished eating, I took my mind away from KY and put my focus back on my friendship with the girls. I praised them and let them know they were the best friends any girl could have.

"I love you girls so much, you've all been my light," I gushed. They have been here, through the three of the hardest times in my life and now the fourth.

When my little brother Jayco died on March 3, 2006, of leukemia, it was hard on us all. April 10, he would have been ten years old; his golden birthday and I won't even be able to put flowers on his grave. I'm leaving for stupid Salem; I guess I will go early this year; he was the little piece of heaven that got me through.

Three years to the day that Jayco had passed, March 3, 2009, I lost my father. He was a firefighter, and he got trapped in a burning building, trying to rescue a little boy who reminded him of Jayco. They told him not to go back in because the building was already collapsing, but he didn't want someone to lose a son like he had lost Jayco he went back in against orders. He never made it back out with the little boy. My heart was crushed like a ton of boulders fell on top of it. When the fire chief came to our door with the news, my mother nearly fainted, and I cried hysterically, and now my mother passes away from cancer on the same day as my dad and Jayco. I felt cursed; I felt a sense of overwhelming anxiety; I wanted to close my eyes and never wake up; I want to run - run far away. My heart has no way of healing the hurt soon, I'm empty.

I wish she would have told me sooner about her terminal illness, that she held bottled inside. It hurt to know I couldn't do anything to make her feel better, and I realize now; she did not inform me of this because of the two heartaches we both have had to suffer in the past few years; she did not want me to worry about her. I am not ready to start my life over in a strange place, especially without her, I'm just not....

Chapter

3

The change

The following day at school turned out to be worse than ever. KY walked towards me, "What do I do - act normal Sandy," I muttered under my breath. I wanted to approach him to try to bring our friendship back up to a calmer situation, but once I got closer to him, I realized he was holding hands with a girl–not just any girl ... but DANIJELA!

"WHAAA," My mind shrieked.

He walked right past me, while Danijela gave me the biggest smirk and tightened her grip on KY's hand like she was clinging to dear life, and KY just ignored me. Just like that, as if I was nothing. As if he never knew me, my heart dropped. He walked away, and I felt hurt he would act like this toward me out of anybody - at least not in my life, when I needed him! My heart dropped in the pit of my stomach, and I realized that I am sort of jealous, I mean I shouldn't be; I told him I only wanted to be friends, so he is free to be with whom he pleases.

I cringed

But come on–Danijela, this made little sense. She is not his type, at all, I think he is with her to make me jealous and–it's working all right.

I couldn't help but notice either; his looks were different–a lot different. He cut off his hair! He has one of those military haircuts, a whole new wardrobe: rocker style, and a new car! I don't know what is going on with him, but I have to admit.... He looks good.... real good. I couldn't help wondering if he is playing hard to get? Or are the tables being turned on me? But I needed to talk to him.

I stopped him in the hallway on our way to lunch. I needed to ask him about the 'new him,' but I didn't want to sound too desperate.

"Hey KY..... nice hair," I joked, he didn't seem to amuse.

"Do you mind if I stop by your house after school today? I want to talk to you,"

Rolling his eyes with annoyance, "Go get a life," he raises his voice, puts on his sunglasses, and walks away, with his hands tucked in the pockets of his ripped jeans, that were laced into his legs, nicely tightened, just right.

Watching him walk away, I wondered thoughtlessly to myself, why the ignorance? Why the disrespect? Did he seriously just say that to me? All these things were running through my head like a tornado, hitting everything in its path, and making a bigger mess than it already was. This is not the KY I know, I don't know what is wrong with him, but I want to know. I leave in a few days, and I would like it if he would get over whatever issue he has, so I can say bye to him as a good friend. I don't want to lose him... so let's see what happens before then.

Although I am still trying to understand the "new" KY, I wondered why Fayth was not at school today. My attention was so focused on KY and dealing with the disaster show with Danijela, I need to be focusing on Fayth, our missing musketeerette.

I called her last night, and she did not answer the phone.

"Jules," I said with worry in my cracked voice, "Try calling Fayth too, see if she picks up."

I tried to focus on my sad looking school lunch

Jules takes her phone out and tries to hide it under her shiny head of hair, "She doesn't pick up," Jules replied, "Maybe she is sick."

"Fayth is never sick," I scolded her for even thinking such a thing.

"Why would you ..." I got mad, "How.... you know Julie, she is never sick!"

"Ok, ok ...calm down, Sands.... I'm sure she is all right," she reassured my pessimistic mind.

"We need to go see if she is home," I demanded to get up from the cafeteria table, "Let's go, come on!"

We skipped the rest of the day, to stop by her house. We needed to find out what was going on. To others, it would be nothing, but to us, we knew something wasn't right, and we had to find out - now. When we arrived at her house, the sky seemed to grow darker, and the clouds rolled in. We immediately hop out of the car, and her mother was sitting on the front porch, holding something and staring into thin air.

We approached the porch with caution, hoping to find Fayth waiting beside her mother.

"Is Fayth home?"

She cried -hysterically. At that point, we knew something was horribly wrong. We repeatedly pushed the question, "Where is Fayth? Is she ok?" and the only thing her mother did was shake her head in disbelief.

"No," with a cracking voice of pain, "Go back to school, girls," she returns inside like someone took her soul.

I would not let her tell us anything. So we stood there banging on the front door,

"Please, Mrs. Kratz–open!"

The door came flinging open

"Fayth was hit by a car last night!…. She's in a coma," she cries as she plops down on the aging wooden porch floor.

"The doctors don't believe she will come out of it," she sighs as her lips quiver. "And…."

We all stood there paralyzed with disbelief waiting for the more bad news that her mother was trying to tell us.

She continues, "… if she does, she will be unable to care for herself."

Those words hit me like rocks in the face. Our hearts sank to the floor, as one of our sisters lay in a hospital bed, and there was nothing we could do about it. Her mother slowly picks herself up and slowly pulls herself into the grief-stricken house. Backing away from the door slowly, every word, every sentence, every conversation that Fayth and I had ever had ran through my mind and

I cried. I couldn't believe what I heard. This couldn't be true–why me, I thought to myself selfishly. I couldn't take anymore; I needed to go see her.

 We rushed as fast as we could to the Hike View Hospital, speeding through traffic in Julie's purple Mustang. Not caring if we got pulled over because getting a speeding ticket was the least of our worries.

 Walking in the long-term care unit-with Fayth's mom, who seemed to have arrived out of nowhere. I had to catch my breath and keep my head up strong as I walked past the hospital rooms where my brother and mother had passed away in. I felt like it froze me in time.

Approaching room 333, there was Fayth, with tubes coming out of her mouth and nose. Head bandaged, with cuts and bruises everywhere. We all wailed.

"I don't want to lose you, Fayth," I whimpered as I clutched her tinder hands, still with flaked glitter purple nail polish.

"This is my fault - I'm cursed."

"Sandy... how could you say something like that?" Alex said with tears in her eyes, grabbing my shoulder and spinning me around towards her.

Pushing her hands from my shoulders and stepping back

"Everyone that gets close to me dies," I yelled at Alex out of sadness, "Is God punishing me for something?"

I look up to the ceiling, and exclaimed to the *man* who I thought had the answers to everything,

"Is this it ... is this what you want for me… to be lonely and hurt!"

"STOP it, Sandra, stop it now!" Fayth's mom scolded me. "This isn't about you, do you understand me…,"

Watching her like a little girl in trouble

"My baby girl is here, in a hospital bed and all you can think about is yourself being cursed, what about me!" she lashed out at me, as we both broke down and sobbed even more.

"I'm sorry, I know…," I repented.

"I need you, Sandra, to be strong ... for me," Fayth's mom began as she lifted my lowered chin and held me tight.

As the lasting embrace continued between Mrs. Kratz and myself, I still selfishly tried to figure out why everyone I loved and cared for was vanishing from my life through death.

We hugged her mother and held Fayth's hand. We prayed that she would wake up and be healthy and happy. I was just waiting for her eyes to move because seeing her like this was heartbreaking and now—reality has set in, that this may be the last time Fayth would be in our lives... forever. I really don't know what to do anymore. Is my life soon to end as well? Only time would tell.

Chapter

4

Fate

Returning home was the hardest part. I didn't want to be there. I tried to go to sleep, but I couldn't. All night, my dreams were of death and curses. My horrid nightmares would comprise everyone around me dying at my feet. All I could do was watch and then a woman standing there in the dark saying, "You will live, and everyone will die, so you can be miserable for the rest of your life to see what it feels like to be banished *mon amour*," and then laughing and disappears. The nightmare woke me up, panting, and sweating. Nothing was making sense anymore.

The Next morning, I didn't want to go to school; I wanted to be by Fayth. She needed me, and I needed to be with her. I felt this overwhelming pull to be by her side. My Uncle Mike excused me from school, he knew Fayth was the most important right now. I met the girls back at Hike View today. She still looks banged up pretty bad, but the doctor says that her vital signs are getting better, and everything seems to be doing abnormally right. Although, he believes that she might not come out from her coma for a while. We would just have to stay positive.

Pulling a chair up to her bed, I got light-headed. I thought maybe this was just the pain and stress of this all. Leaning into her ear, I spill my heart,

"I'm not sure how I can manage to lose another person close to me," I whispered to Fayth, trying to hold back my tears, "Jayco, my dad, my mom, and now you ... laying in the hospital ... in a coma. My emotions are on an all-time high," I continue, "and they're spiraling out of control, Fayth.... I don't know what to do.... don't leave me ...Please," as I kiss her hand, and tears roll down my face.

 I look up from Fayth's bedside, as I hear someone creeping in–it was KY, holding daisies. He walked over to the bed and sat them down on the dresser.

"Hey...," his voice trembled, "How is she doing?"

Wiping my eyes, "Good," through the tears, "the doctor says that her vital signs are good, but she still hasn't opened her eyes," I responded to him with still a grudge in my voice. I stood there staring at Fayth but could feel his eyes burning through me.

"Sandy?"

I looked up from Fayth once more and made contact with his beautiful blue eyes. I felt the butterflies flutter through my stomach, then quickly look away.

"I'm no longer seeing Danijela," He walked to me from the other side of the bed, "I apologize for acting how I was acting; I never meant for anything to get in between our friendship," he hesitated while looking at the floor, "I..... I haven't been myself lately–Forgive me, Sandy?", He says as he grabs my waist and pulls me towards him.

"KY... I," I breathe him in, "I can't ...," I explained to him I only wanted his friendship, but he cut me off; probably afraid that I would tell him we couldn't be together.

"Please Sandy–I want you," he begged, "I need you, I've been thinking about you every day, I can't get you out of my head," His body becomes hot

"It's weird ...I have these feelings running through my body that I can't control," he ends the plea.

I looked away from him because his eyes were so breathtaking, that I felt if I continued to look at him, he would convince me that being with him was the right thing to do. "I accept your apology KY but don't do that to me again... okay?" I stressed to him, "I have too much in my life now to deal with you being a shitty friend."

"I promise," he says as his face lights up and he picks me up into the air and spins me around.

I chuckle as he sets me down, with his calm, gentle touch.

"Hey...can we go on a 'FATE?' He asks with the reassurance that I knew what that meant.

"A FATE?" I questioned with severe curiosity in his choice of words.

"Yes, a FATE ...a friendship date," He explained, "We can go to the Skate Ring food or something."

"Fine ... sure,"

I agreed to this *FATE'* but reassured him we were going as friends. He promised me we would go as friends and leave it at that. He asked if I needed a ride home, and he'd be more than happy to take me back.

"I bet you would," I joked as I agreed he could. As we walked away, still with our hands intertwined, his hands were so hot and sweaty...... but super soft to the touch, I loved his warmth.

I felt good ....that ...you know.....we were *friends* again.

Never being able to say goodbye is a hard concept to accept. I love this girl with all my heart, and I will continue to keep her in my thoughts. I want to see her pretty, pale, green eyes before I leave. My heart's been hurting like a heart attack, and no one knows what kind of pain I have been going through lately.

Yes, I'm selfish, I know, but that is how my mind was processing all of this.

I just want the best for everyone in my life, so I will give them the best, and treat them well because I am leaving in a few more days, and want no regrets.

BUT on another good note, Fayth is doing better. Ever since we started showing up to the hospital, the doctor says her overall health is improving... drastically.

"I have never seen this kind of healing before," The doctor said, astonished.

I joked that it must be the power of friendship.

"Or maybe you girls are just witches," he joked and chuckled while walking away; I stared at the doctor, with confusion. The joke wasn't that funny, I have heard that word a lot lately.

I laughed and mumbled to myself, "Witches?"

I stared at Fayth and wondered... What if?

I surely didn't want to leave for Salem if Fayth was still in the hospital; I would feel horrible if I went, and she was to come out from her coma, and I was not there to greet her. I grew angrier at the thought. Holding her hand, "I'm here." The following day I called KY to make sure we were still on for our *'FATE.'* I was really excited as I waited for him to pick up.

I called

"What!" An agitated voice answered.

I had to look down at my cell phone to make sure I was calling the right person.

"Ky?" I reluctantly asked.

"What!" Again he responds, sounding more irritated.

"Are we still on for tonight?" I asked with caution and sadness.

"I'm not sure, I'll call you!" as he hung up the phone with such force, my ears vibrated.

What the hell was that? I couldn't believe what just happened, and I felt more hurt than ever because he promised me he wouldn't treat me like this again. I am leaving and don't want to feel like I owe him anything. I think I will call our friendship quits because I cannot deal with his mood swings. During tonight's get together, I will let him know we can't be friends anymore.

Tonight was our *FATE*….. BUT AAHHHH……. I cannot believe the stunt that KY pulled this evening. He was supposed to pick me up at 6:00 pm, and when 7 o'clock rolled around, I called him. He answered his phone with an attitude like I was the one who was late!

I raised my voice with him in disgust, "Where are you, are you still coming!"

"Meet me there," he scolded and hung up the phone. I was still kinda ticked off, but I decided to go, anyway. I mean, what is one more horrendous moment in my life... right?

When I got to the restaurant, it was already 7:45 pm. I got us a table and waited, waited, and…... waited

"What the…..?" as I checked my watch to keep myself sane. I waited until 9:00 pm! He never showed!

I tried to call him but he did not answer his phone. I am genuinely, deeply hurt, I thought this would strengthen our friendship. I guess he doesn't care about this friendship as I do. Forget it then, I am done; I am wiping my hands clean, time to move on and out!

"I do not want to stress over this boy anymore," I huffed as I was preparing myself to leave home.

As soon as I left the restaurant, I called Julie.

"Jules, I'm coming to pick you up, let's go grab something to eat, I am starving," I demanded of her.

"Sure, I'll get ready," she said without hesitation.

I had to tell her what happened.

Picking Julie up from her house, I bet she could sense the tension in my car from inside her house. As I told her the story, I continued on and on, you could see the disgust in her eyes; she could not believe what I was telling her.

As I explained the rest of the story, she exploded with anger, "Let's go over there right now! I will give him a piece of my mind!"

"No, Jules...... let's leave it like this," I reminded her. I really do not want to have anything to do with him ever again! I don't need a friend like him in my life, I thought this was something new, but I thought wrong.

Talk about mood swings! I have not talked to KY for a few days, and out of the blue, he called me as nothing had happened!

Can you believe him!

What nerve does he have?

I yelled at him, telling him how he stood me up and did not even have the decency to call me, saying he would not be there, or even the next day after the fact!

Ha! I feel so stupid for even giving him another chance to hurt me, I feel so naïve. After I gave him a piece of my mind, I hung up the phone so hard, I accidentally broke it by slamming it on my countertops. I was in my feelings to the max; I felt like the world stopped like I was being pushed to the side, I felt like absolute SHIT! I love too hard to be treated like this.

About an hour after that incident happened, the front doorbell rang. My heart sank and could only imagine what other horrible news I could possibly get, at this point in my life, I was past being optimistic and slowly churning my soul to be a pessimist. I answered the door to a beautiful bouquet of white roses, all crisp and clean-cut. Standing behind those roses was….. KY.

"Hi Sandra," he said with his puppy dog blue eyes.

Looking at him with such hurt

"Go away Ky," I said blasting at him, as I went to slam the door

in his face but catching it with his foot,

" Please?" he begged as he glared into my eyes. - damn him.

I would not accept these roses; I was adamant about that because

me taking those, was me accepting the cruel way he had treated

me, he did not deserve my friendship.

"I really don't want to speak with you," I pushed the matter,

holding the door firm

"Sandy…. Please," his voice became stern, and he pushed my

front door open with one hand.

An unsettling feeling overcame my body, so I listened to his

pathetic stories, just because I felt sorry for him.

Walking into the living, I felt his breath on my neck, and my

neck hairs stood up. It was not a sweet feeling; it felt - weird.

He sat the roses down on the coffee table as we sat on my couch

sofa. He got closer to me, as I rested into the couch.

"Are you coming to my birthday party tomorrow?" he asked with excitement as he laid his hand on my leg.

"Probably not," As I pushed his hand away, which seemed to be boiling.

Staring at him with nervousness, I finally had to let him know he cannot come and make everything all right whenever he wants. Getting up from the couch and walking to the hallway, I turn around to him, "You know KY, friendships don't work like this."

Getting up to follow me, he continued to beg me, like a puppy begging for his bone,

"**PLEASE** come to my party, I need you there, Sandy."

Taking a deep breath to gather my thoughts,

"I will….." feeling slightly bad for him for sounding somewhat pathetic, "under one condition," I argued.

"What is that?" He questioned with a smirk on his face.

"That you would *never* treat me like this again!" as if this wasn't repeated already.

"I promise you," he said, grabbing my hands with his hot ones while staring me in the eyes, "I plead to you, Sandy, just come." Finishing up our conversation, I let KY know it was time for him to go, I couldn't stand looking in his beautiful eyes any longer, he has a hold on my weak soul. He kissed me on the cheek, and we said our goodbyes.

Closing the door as he walked away, I didn't know what I felt... I felt... like I was being manipulated by his caring words. I swear he is worse than a girl PMSing.

Waking up the next day, was sure to brighten my spirit, today was the day that Fayth was discharged from the hospital. Julie, Alex, and I all went to welcome her home and make sure she was comfortable. We told her how much we were worried that she would not wake up, and I was all over the place because four big people in my life would have been gone.

"Thank you, baby Jesus, you are here with us, healthy, and doing well," we cried and laughed to her with my sense of humor, mixed with madness.

"You know something, girls?" Fayth began.

"What," we all said with curiosity as we smiled and got closer.

"The whole time I was in the coma, I could hear you all!" she exclaimed with a smile on her face.

How relieved we were to know she knew she would be all right.

"I'm glad the four musketeers are together before I leave on Thursday," I whimpered to the girls, looking pale. I explained to them how I received a call from my "aunt" Gertrude and how she did not seem welcoming and sounded weird.

"Sandy, you're overreacting," Fayth says and giggles, "and when you get there, you should give this lady a try."

"Yeah, after all, she stepped up and took responsibility for you," Alex interrupts and reassures me.

Still, I don't want to be around someone who will treat me like a little girl, I will be 16 on April 28th. I do not want to feel smothered; I want to feel free, all the mess that is stirred into my life, I need to breathe. I hope she is prepared, this will not be a smooth transition for me, and I don't plan on making it any better for her.

Was I acting immature? - Sure

But I have my reason, okay.

Getting back home from the hospital, I was so full of energy. I walked into the house, humming a beautiful tone. I needed those positive vibes in my life, and knowing one of my best friends is okay; it just kept me smiling. I was even excited to get ready for KY's party. Although a part of me is telling me to *STAY AWAY* from him, I have a soft spot for him and don't feel these feelings ending soon.

As I arrived at KY's party, I felt…. unwelcome but pushing those fears aside, I got a glimpse of KY from across the room I make my way over to him, holding a small boxed present, I reach up to give him a hug when someone yanked my arm back, "What are you doing here?", A crude, nasty voice said.

Ugh…my eardrums broke.

I turned around to the face of bright, pink lip-stick wanna-be

Barbie doll- Danijela!

Standing there like she was a life-size beach bimbo or something.

"I was invited….. isn't that right KY," I forcefully pushed the

words out of my mouth, making sure she understood them

clearly.

"By who?" as she went over to KY, kissing him, with no respect

for herself, and groped him.

KY did nothing - but say, "Thanks for coming."

Staring at him in utter, morbid disbelief.

"Thanks for coming,…..thanks for coming!" I screamed in my

head.

Was he serious! My mind was running with swirls around my

head like I had just got hit with a dose of vertigo.

AHHHHHH, I should have given him thanks for coming… right

in his face, I muttered to myself as I walked away.

What a real piece of work was all I could fumble through my

brain.

I stayed a little longer and enjoy myself with the girls, whom I had met up with at the party, and after a while, I questioned that decision and my sanity. I got uncomfortable because Danijela would grope KY like they were in private and kiss him while staring at me, ugh… I couldn't take it anymore and decided I wanted to go home.

"I'm going to go, girls," I said to my small pack.

"No! Stay!" Fayth begged.

"I'm tired - I need to finish packing anyway…..you girls stay, enjoy the party, I think I need alone time anyway," I reassured them I'd be okay.

I wasn't lying, my plane leaves at 8:00 o'clock tomorrow morning, I had more than enough crap to deal with, I needed to calm my mind.

As I stormed out the front door and down the paved walkway, KY came running after me, he grabbed my arm with such force, that I felt like I was flying backward.

"Sandra, why are you leaving?" He raised his voice and demanded an answer on my departure.

"Ow ...KY", my face said it all, let me go," I struggled to rip my arm back from his clenched clutches, "you're hurting me!" I cried to him while ripping back my fanciful severed limb, as I walked faster.

A show of witnesses was forming.

"Why are you leaving me!" he yelled at me, trying to catch up to my glide, suddenly grabbing my shoulders back to turn me around to face his.

"I'm done playing your little games KY," snatching my arm from him again, fixing my blouse, that loosened, "I am younger than you *AND* act more mature than you," I beat into him, "I thought you wanted this friendship to grow, but obviously you are still a little boy who needs to grow up," I exclaimed!

"I don't want to be friends anymore, KY....sorry!" I yelled at him, turning back away to leave.

He grabs me again, "Sandy..."

"Let me go!" I shout to him, "I never want to see you, again....

EVER!"

Pushing him back, sweat dripped from his face, like he was

standing in hell, his eyes lit up BRIGHT RED!!!

No, not some made-up saying ...like LITERALLY!

I backed up in disbelief. I could not believe what I had just seen!

"Are you ok?" I said with a crackling voice.

"YES! I'm fine; I think you should leave NOW!" he turns

himself in a hurry. As he walked away, I swear, I saw smoke

coming from his body! Not knowing what to think, my mind was

confused.

Were my eyes playing tricks on me, or was I tired?

The crowd dispersed, and I felt an awkward chill going through

my body, I needed to get out of here.

Almost running to my car, I had Goosebumps flying through my

body as I came out of a horror movie. I rushed home as fast as I

could, thinking about what I had just seen. Still a little confused

and dismayed, I made it home safely. I hope KY doesn't show up tomorrow, I feel, like he has me in a trance or something. I just need to get away from him! After tonight, I think this was my last straw!

Chapter

5

The Departure

The dreaded day is finally here, today marks a new chapter in my life. One that is sure to be an adventure. I am glad *my girls* came with me to the airport; there was nothing, I wanted more than to see their beautiful faces before I left. We arrived at the airport super early, so we could spend as much time as possible with each other, with no worries. We talked, and we cried; we gushed, and we squealed like piglets. People were looking at us like we were crazy, but we didn't care, all we cared about was that we were with each other. They didn't want to see me go, and I didn't want to leave.

"This is it," I said holding back my tears, as the intercom called for my flight that was boarding, "I'm going to a new town and will have to make new friends, but no one will ever come close to you guys," we grouped circled hugged and said our goodbyes.

I never spoke with KY before I left, and I hope he doesn't call because I do not want to deal with his nonsense. My head was still spinning from the night before, and I was trying to make sense of this all, but maybe it was something I wasn't meant to know. Perhaps, it was a lesson that I have yet to understand, but at this moment in time, and I'm okay with that.

My girls told me with reassurance, "We will not tell him you left," they pinkie promised, although I think Julie may say something because she has always wanted us to become a couple for the longest time,

"Oh Julie, can you not keep a secret for nothing," I thought to myself with sarcasm.

I kissed them all once more, appreciating their embrace, not wanting to let go.

"Sandy, hurry," my Uncle Mike called, "You will miss your flight."

"Wouldn't that be nice," I whispered to the girls, as they giggled through my sarcasm. I walked to my Uncle Mike and gave him a big hug.

"You'll be fine, Sands," he says as he rubs the top of my head like I was a baby.

"Says the guy that is living the life," I removed his calloused hands from my head.

"Love ya, kid," he smiles.

I smirked and walked to my flight doors, not wanting to look back because I might just run away. I took a deep breath "Let's do this," I quietly whispered to myself.

The flight was four and a half hours, and we have half an hour left to go before we make it to Salem. I am kind of nervous; I do not know what to say to Gertrude when I meet her, or how she will look. Will she look like my mother? Will her prominent features be a reflection of what I am leaving behind? Do I prepare for the worse and accept the change, why must I be so pessimistic right now?

BUT Oh God, I hope not! I mean, I could not deal with looking at a lady that resembles my beloved mother; this would just crush me and make me want to break down.

Chapter

6

Hello Salem

Stepping off of the plane was a sigh of relief, but I also still felt nervous, I stumble as I take in the scenery. I look around, trying to find a sign with my name on it. Standing on my tippy-toes trying to reach my 5'1" body frame above the hoards of people at the airport. I turn around to glimpse the horizon behind me, just as a tall, pale, leather-skinned man, in a black suit approaches me.

"Ms. Garcia.... my name is Patrick, please follow me this way," his deep stretched voice lingers, as he turns sluggishly to walk away.

"Ms. Garcia?" This guy sounds like a mummy and looks like he is from the afterlife.

"Is Gertrude waiting outside?" I asked, trying to look around to his face.

"Madame Galva is awaiting at her fortress for your arrival."

"Madame? Awaiting? Fortress?" It's not the 1800s anymore, I said to myself as I rolled my eyes and mouthed, "Ok."

"How nice of my aunt to have someone else pick me. What a great welcome," I said sarcastically as we walked outside. Staring at me with not such an amused look, he continued to walk outside, stiff arms straight at his side I followed this cold man out to a limo, "Wow," I said aloud, "She must be loaded," I giggled, as I stepped inside.

Driving through town, the limo I was riding in seemed to get stares and glares like it was not welcomed. My stomach twisted with anxiety, as we drove to the edge of town, turning down Bark Creek Rd. There were tons of broken, slightly scary looking trees, crows, and even wolves! All of which seem to stare right through the black tinted windows into me. It seemed like the day had turned to night, and it was only one o'clock in the afternoon. Pulling up to huge, black, the old house was only the beginning.

"Is this her house?" I said eagerly.

"Yes," Patrick responded coldly, his voice seemed to linger.

It still amazed my eyes, this house looked like it had been here for centuries but still had some kind of beautiful life to it. As we pulled into the driveway, I opened the limo door to a well kept front lawn.

"Go in the house," my new mummy murmured, "Madame Galva is awaiting your presence," Patrick roughly pronounced.

"Go in the house, Madame Galva is awaiting your presence," I mocked under my breath.

"I'll bring in your belongings," with his long-lasting tone.

Heading towards the front door which seemed like days, brushing past bush after bush, while finally reaching this marvelous wooden red oak door with perfectly engraved words on it that read in French:

"Avec arches d'or, et les ailes creuses,

un seul qui veut, peut rêver"

("With golden arches, and hollow wings, only one who wishes,

can dream")

Now I took French class in school, so I could read it entirely; however, who would want this on their door? I questioned myself with confusion. Going for the doorknob, it seemed to open…. all by itself.

"Huh," I thought, "This needs to be fixed." trying to amuse myself from the weird display of confusion.

As the door opens, I can smell that the house has powerful odors, like herbs, lakes, flowers, cats, a bit of everything, if you ask me. Walking past the doorway, I hear a voice from the back saying, "come in, my darling Sands, I'm in the kitchen."

"Here We Go Again with the Sands," I quietly whispered under my breath, this time I will let her know to call me Sandra, **NOT** Sands.

Walking towards the kitchen, I saw everything in the house looked kind of worn out and old, there were early portraits on the wall and spider webs on the ceiling. As I walked toward the bright light coming from the kitchen, foul-smelling odors continued to fill the air in the house like Thanksgiving Day, except this was no turkey. I had to plug my nose; the senses were too strong; I gagged just a bit.

Turning in the kitchen doorway, there was this *beautiful* woman. She looked like a porcelain doll. Like in the portraits on the wall. She had long black hair running down her incredible toned back with white marble bangs. Her eyes; she had the most beautiful eyes I had ever seen, cat-like eyes, bright green with a bit of grey and gold speckles in them, never have I ever seen anything like that before in my life - amazing. She was wearing a black gown that looks so elegant to be worn around the house for casual attire with black ankle boots. Kind of stylish…I liked it. Staring at me with her cat eyes, she says,

" You look just like your mother," kissing me on the forehead, and pulling out a chair, "take a seat."

"Welcome, my darling Sands," her words seem to stay on her lips.

Interrupting her respectfully, "I'm sorry," I started, "but could you please call me Sandra or Sandy,"

"It's just that….. Well, I don't know you, and you really don't know me, for you to call me my short nickname, that only my mother and father called me."

"Certainly, my dear," she sighed, "Communication is key," She continues stirring her tea that seemed to appear out of nowhere on the darken hardwood table.

"So…. what are you cooking," my curious mouth began, "and is it… dinner," I asked with all honesty while grunting my nose. She laughed gently, "No, sweetie, it's a secret family recipe." She never told me what her 'secret recipe' was for, but I could not imagine what you could use such a rancid formula for, perhaps, to kill mice.

As a mouse scurried across the floor

We talked, and she explained to me that we had much to do, and no time should be wasted. I was kind of confused, I did not know what she was talking about and could only imagine what kind of 'things' could be done.

I mean, the house was absolutely spotless, well except for the spider webs on the ceiling, so there was no cleaning needed to be done. I was wondering if it was my room that needed to be fixed up.

"So, can I see my room?" excitedly, I asked.

"Of course, darling, I believe Patrick is done fixing and unpacking your things," she said, with calmness, while turning her back to rest her dainty black mug on the countertop.

"What!" I thought in my head this whole time, he was going through my things, and I did not understand, "I hope this isn't a habit."

"Let's go, my dear."

Following the hallway to the flower paintings that filled the walls. I was taking in every bit of this experience. The walls seemed to come alive, the term, *'the walls are listening'* seemed more real than fantasy talk in here.

"Stay close, my dear," she breaths, "I do not want you to get lost," she said sarcastically with a chuckle.

Walking up this narrow, spiral staircase, I was then led down a deep, dark hallway full of ancient life. The art on the walls continued to dance through this almost *magical* area. I followed closely behind Gertrude. Arriving at a vast, beautiful room behind a massive wooden door, the room seemed to draw me in. I felt an overwhelming sense that I was supposed to be there, I turned to Gertrude,

"This is mine?" I asked her with stars in my eyes as I made my way inside the room, touching the dark mahogany armoire that laid against the wall.

"But of course, dear, only the best, for my niece, "She responded with pleasure in her eye.

I could not believe my eyes; I guess this might not be so bad after all.

"I will let you get settled in, dinner will be ready in a half-hour, "She continued. Shutting my bedroom door quietly, I was still feeling nervous as I walked over to my bed. In a way, I felt *'at home'* because I had my bed with me, at least from back home. I knew I would sleep comfortably tonight, at least.

Lying down on my bed, I was thinking about *my girls* back home.

"I should call them," I said to myself.

As I went to grab my phone from my back pocket, I noticed the screen was broken, what luck I have.

"Shit.. this suck," I said out loud, "I guess I will have to go get a new cell phone tomorrow."

"Sandy," I hear Gertrude in the distance, "Dinner is ready, my dear."

"Coming," I replied, putting my phone back in my pocket.

I made my way down the hallway, being curious as I was. While examining the beautifully decorated walls, I passed a black cat who seemed to look into my soul. I am highly allergic to cats, but for some reason, this cat did not make me sneeze. It was strange, but I brushed it off as nervousness in a new place.

Finally, reaching the kitchen, with hunger, I proceeded to ask Gertrude, "How many cats do you have?"

"Oh my dear, tons, they come and go as they please, with an exception to Jasper. He likes to lounge around the house," she said.

"That wouldn't be the black cat upstairs," I smiled with curiosity.

"Yes….. yes, that would be him," she smiled, "did he scare you, my darling?" she laughed.

"He startled me a little, but I could manage his ferociousness," I exclaimed with touches of sarcasm, actually able to make a joke after all.

We both chuckled.

"Why do you ask, sweetie?"

"It's because I'm allergic to cats, and when he came by me, I didn't sneeze."

"Oh," Gertrude nervously let's out, "well - he's a…..special cat *orrr* it might just be the breed of cat he is, no worries," She said this with nervousness in her voice, "LET'S eat."

She served me my bowl of soup that looked as bad as it probably tasted.

"What is this?" I asked her with disgust.

"Frog eye and leg soup," She said delightedly, "my favorite."

Holding back my vomit and my horrible gag reflex.

"Gertrude, no disrespect to your cooking because I'm sure you love it and all, but is there a burger place around here," I asked with all honesty.

"Oh, of course, dear," her delighted face turned upside down, "I'm sorry to rush you into this kind of food," she sounded disappointed.

"I'll have Patrick take you to Burger Palace if you like?"

"Do you mind if I go alone," I asked.

"Are you sure you're ready to walk around alone in this town," she gasped.

"Yeah, I know not to go with strangers," I said eagerly and sarcastically.

"Ok," she says, "Standing up from the kitchen table and walking to the back door, with a few pairs of keys hung, selecting a pair. "Take my car."

"Oh, thanks," wide-eyed, "but I was going to walk; it's not far, is it?"

"No, but I don't want you to walk around here alone," she smiles, "Plus the Mercedes has a navigation system," she moves her chiseled shoulders up and smiles.

"The Mercedes?" I choked.

This house is an ancient pile of wood, but she has a brand new Mercedes. I was a little bewildered, but whatever I thought to myself, I get to drive a Mercedes.

Leaving out the front door and making my way to the side of the house, I approached the Mercedes with caution; I was so nervous I would scratch it by looking at it. It was so shiny and beautiful, black on black. Getting in, I rubbed the leather seats, I slowly put the key in the ignition. It purred like a kitten.

Leaving the driveway with attentiveness, there was that damn cat again, just staring at me with his beady little, yellow eyes. I honked the horn for him to move, but he just walked towards the car, like a model on the catwalk (pun intended).

"Ah, what do you want now?" I said with irritation as I got out of the car. Making sure not to run him over. Walking around the car, he seemed to have vanished.

"Ok, I must be that crazy," I said, confused as I hopped back in the car, still trying to figure out..... where'd he went too.

Finally, driving into the evening bliss, I turned on the navigation system; I wanted to clear my head. Driving through town, admiring the old town life. I broke down in hard tears and cried.

"I can't believe I lost my mother, the only person I had left in my family; I do not know how I will make it," whimpering to myself. Suddenly, I felt a light breeze, and a soft familiar voice faintly whispers, "Honey, I'm here."

Hitting the brakes with my all strength, turning my head in all kinds of directions,

"What the hell was that!?"

"Now, I know I'm going crazy," I said aloud.

It sounded like my mother's voice; I swear it sounded just like her; maybe I imagined it because I want her back so bad.

After calming myself down, I continued to follow the navigation system, pulling into Burger Palace, still shook up by the voice I heard. "Was that really, my mother?" I thought. I quickly shook that idea out of my head. I don't believe in ghosts or anything like that. It was just my imagination. I kept reassuring myself and tried to press those thoughts out of my mind.

Pulling up to this red building, with a fake moat that had fishes swimming it in, sitting on top, in big golden letters read *'Burger Palace.'*

"This must be it," I said sarcastically to myself as I stepped out onto the black wet pavement, which they must have just cleaned. Walking into Burger Palace, there was this group of teenagers; about three girls, and five guys all sitting around a booth table, they all seemed to just stare at me like a freak at a circus. Gliding past them, to get to the counter. Looking at the menu, deciding on what to get, a dulcet voice from behind me says,

"Try the King Burger," slowly turning around to this gorgeous, Deep-blue eyed black-haired, face like it was carved from the heavens and sent down just for me. I lost my breath for a second. Just staring at him, he repeated, "You should try the King Burger, it's my favorite."

"Oh, um yeah…. sure," said nervously as I chuckled to re-gather my endless thoughts of wonder.

"Two King Burgers," he ordered, handing him a 10 dollar bill.

"Oh no, it is okay, I can pay for my own food."

"No, I am a gentleman," he stares at me, "a gentleman never makes a lady pay," speaking with his beautiful blue eyes.

"If you insist," I chuckled, wondering if chivalry is still alive in this town.

"No ketchup, extra pickles," I told the cashier who looked annoyed at the thought of puppy love that seemed to form in front of him.

Holding out his hand, he says,

"My name is Cole - Cole Creek.... I haven't seen you around town before."

"Oh, I'm new actually, just got in today," I responded, as his group of friends stared at me with cheesy smiles on their faces.

"What's your name?" he asked with precaution, staring deep into my eyes.

"Sandra.....," I cleared my throat, "Sandy," with butterflies in my stomach. I haven't felt this way in a while.

"Well.... Sandy, would you like to join my friends and me" He gently asked as he made a semi-bow movement towards his table.

"Oh no, I'm so sorry, I really have to get going," I told him with disappointment.

"Well, when can I see you again?" he questioned, "Are you going to Salem High?"

"No, not now, my aunt will home-school me until I start my junior year," I explained to him.

"Too bad," he stated while trying to possess me with his mind while maintaining eye contact, "I was looking forward to walking you to class."

My face got red like a fresh cherry.

"I really have to get going….. Cole?" I pretend to forget his name, but all of me know that was a false statement, "maybe we'll see each other around," I said, shuffling out the door, with my food in my hands.

"Yeah, maybe we will," he said, watching me leave Burger Palace from the door.

Walking out, I noticed Coel just staring out the window at me, hands in his front pocket with a slight slough to his rugged demeanor. I think I'm in lust! I couldn't stop smiling, a grin on my face from ear to ear.

"Keeping walking…..keeping walking," I began in my head, "Don't look back,…...keep forward."

I looked

I smile and tuck my hair behind my ear as he raises one hand while the other still neatly tucked in his pants.

HE WAS BEAUTIFUL; I have someone to look forward to seeing around this town! I don't think I want to be homeschooled anymore.

Arriving back at Gertrude's house, I had seen her standing at the window, walking up to the front door, there was that damn cat again! Shooing it from the door, he gazed into my eyes before running off.

"That cat is so weird,"

As I stepped through the front door, the door slammed behind me.

"I don't remember it being windy out," chuckling at Gertrude, who was standing there staring at me like ice.

"Did you find everything okay?" she questioned.

"Yes, I met some kids from town, over there," I set my food down on the living room coffee table.

"How cool," she tried to mock my stance, "but it would have been nice if you called and told me you were okay," she snapped at me.

"Sorry, but my phone is broke, and I can't answer," I snapped back.

"Tomorrow, we'll go into town and get you a new one after your schoolwork," she said.

"Cool, no problem…. ok well it's late, I'm going to go up to my room and eat," I yawned.

She told me goodnight and just watched me walk up the stairs like a prisoner.

"What's up with her?" I huffed to myself.

Today was a brand new day! I woke up refreshed and ready to roll. A knock on my door woke up my ears to the day.

"Ready to go," Gertrude said through the door.

"Give me 5," I got up to start my first home-school lesson of the day. I couldn't concentrate on this stuff all I could think about was...Cole…. Cole Creek, I daydreamed away, I couldn't stop thinking of him. Time seemed to fly, my world seemed to stand still, and my thoughts could only focus on his breathtaking looks and his angelic voice. I needed to see him- I HAD to see him again.

"Sandy?" a snap of the fingers in my face woke me up, "Hello - we're done."

Snapping out of the trance I was in, trying to get my focal point back on Gertrude.

"Did you learn anything today?" Gertrude cringed a bit.

"We're done?" I cross-questioned the lessons with a chuckle.

"Honestly, I couldn't focus today, "I said with a smile on my face.

"Well, you were daydreaming," Gertrude adds to my debate, "So I guess we're done for the day."

"Let's go to town!" she burst out while slamming her lesson book closed.

Heading out the door, I was hit with mixed emotions, and KY came to my mind. Ugh, why must my mind curse me? I needed to get my mind off of KY; I needed to start anew. I needed - I don't know what I need honestly. I'll figure it out as I go

 Finally, I headed into town, Gertrude, and I went out and about today after a long grueling homeschooling lesson. She needed to pick up some groceries, and I needed a new cell phone. We first went to go get my phone, but when we walked into the *Cellular Heaven* store, Gertrude seemed to get a lot of stares from people. I mean, she was wearing Skinny Black Jeans, with Black high heels, a Blacktop that bared her midriff, black scarf around her head, and black shades, but I thought it was very *'diva'* of her. I did not see anything wrong with it, but that's just me.

"Look around, darling, anything you want, you can get whatever you want….only the best for my niece" she sounded like money was not an object.

As I looked around, they started to stare at me too, like I had tree limbs coming out of my nose or something. Turning to the lady standing next to me that had been staring at me without embarrassment, I quickly asked, "Can I help you?".

She gave me a huff, set the object in her hands down, and walked away.

Walking back toward Gertrude, who happened to be watching, I questioned,

"What was all that about?".

"People just don't understand good taste, that's all," she explained to me with laughter in her voice, while looking back to the ladies that were gawking, "Did you find something you like?".

 Showing her the latest Apple iPhone, I said, "Yup, right here."

"Excellent choice, my darling," nodding.

At the checkout, no one seemed to want to help us, ringing the customer service bell, "Hello, we're readying to check out," I established our presence at the counter. At last, we get a cashier who also seemed to have more than an attitude...almost like fear.

"Is this it!", she rudely said, while trying to avoid eye contact.

"Yes, sweetie," Gertrude kindly replied with a broad smile on her face, "But you know you should be nicer to people, you never know what they can do," pointing her finger in a twirling motion, as she winks, while glaring at the girl, who seemed to have peed her pants. We paid her and left, I was trying to get out of there as fast as I could.

"I hate rude people," I began exclaiming.

"It is okay darling; someday she will get what is coming to her, our karmic actions speak louder than anything we do in our lives - one day you'll understand my sweets," she tittered, "now to the grocery store."

"I would like to pick some food out too if you don't mind," I asked.

"Of course, dear," she replied with certainty, "My house is your house now," she pawed my cheek.

Getting in her blacked-out Mercedes, my mind is still running wild, I feel so much anxiety and nervousness, but I feel happy. I think more and more drawn to this place, the more I am here. We begin driving down Coldwell Ave. When something pulled me to look out my window, it was Coel!

He was walking down the street with his friends, looking oh-so-very cute.

"Oh, I see you have a crush," Gertrude said with a smirk on her face.

"What? Huh? I didn't say anything," I replied, extremely embarrassed while trying to focus my attention on something else.

"You didn't have to, I can see it all over your face," with a caring voice, "You know, be careful about finding love too soon, and live a little bit, the first sweetie."

While trying to take the embarrassing questions from myself, I asked Gertrude out of curiosity.

"Have you ever been married?"

"Oh yes, darling, a long time ago; it did not work out, and we were forced to call it quits," with sorrow in her voice.

"Oh... I'm sorry, I never meant to bring up any bad memories for you," I apologized.

"The past is the past, and now we must live for the future," she said with a sad smile.

"Can I ask you another question," I nervously asked.

"Of course, anything you want to know or hear, I am here for you," she glanced at me.

"Do you have any kids?" I guess this struck a nerve because she changed the subject fast.

"Let's talk about something else shall we,"

Her face seemed to go blue with sadness, and she looked like she might have passed out if her mind didn't wander somewhere new. I felt horrible for asking her such a heart-wrenching question that obviously drove a stake in her heart.

Pulling up to *Grocery Mart,* "We're here... let's go," she sighed.

Walking into the store, it was the same ordeal as the *Cellular Heaven* store. Stares and glares, snickers, and whispers.

"What is with the people in this town? Do they not have manners or something?"I asked myself.

We did not stay in there for long, we were only basically here for me because Gertrude said she goes to a unique store for her *'real'* ingredients. I was confused as to what *'real'* was but did not want to bombard her with tons of questions, so I left it at that but could only imagine, as the memories of the frog eye soup, flashed in my head, I shivered.

Arriving at this store, that was well hidden behind trees, and scary stringy bushes, dark, and gloomy fog seemed to surround the store.

I interrogated Gertrude, "What is this place?"

She just smiled, "Wait here."

As she left the car and walked towards the store, I noticed a few women standing in the window, staring at me. I was getting a little freaked out.

A few moments later, Gertrude walked out, holding a black paper bag, with what looked to be a *witch's hat* on it. Gertrude entered the car, not saying a word, and we drove off.

I wondered to myself, what could have been in that store? But most importantly, what is in that bag? During the entire car ride back to the house, Gertrude and I said not one word to each other. The vibe in the car changed, and I felt uncomfortable, and everything just felt uneasy.

Pulling up to the house, it seemed different. Patrick was standing in the doorway, staring at the car like it was the morgue, coming to get him or something. Patrick came over to my side of the car, opening the door and helping me out.

"Thanks, Pat," I mumbled.

He just stared at me, like he was trying to send me a message about something, but it was still unclear. Going over to Gertrude's side, he slowly opens up her door, and they make a weird, kind of eye contact.

I just stood there looking around. This town seems like the heart of a zombie town, not the Salem witch trials, as I was scared into thinking such a thought. Remembering that I wanted to get more information on it, I'd figured I'd ask Gertrude a question or two.

Noticing that Patrick and Gertrude already walked in the house, I scrambled in after them.

"Gertrude," I said, as I ran through the front door.

"Yes, my dear," she hesitated as she turned around with that black bag still in her hand, clutched on for dear life.

"Were the Salem Witch trials real?"

She darted me a look, which sent shivers down my spine. I thought to myself, how I regretted asking that question for some reason.

"Yes, but of course, my dear, the greatest and most tragic events to have ever cursed this town," she defensively responded, "Why?".

"Just wondering," trying to avoid eye contact, "well I'm going to head upstairs….it's been a long day, and I'm going to mess with my new phone", I fumbled to tell her.

She just turned her back to me without a word but not without a Gerty glance through her piercing eyes; she walked away into a frigid looking door that leads to a back room,

"Was that door there before?" I doubted my mind.

Walking into the back room, with the black bag she brought

home and seemed to disappear for the night.

How my curiosity was taking control and was on an all-time

high, I couldn't help but wonder……..

Chapter

7

Witch?

While walking towards the staircase, I couldn't help but glance back at the door, Gertrude had just disappeared into.

"I didn't remember seeing this door yesterday," I once again questioned my sanity. The door looked like it came from a castle or something, big, bulky, and creepy beautiful looking, not your average, *go to the local hardware store* and buy a door, kind of a door. I mean, it kind of freaked me.

Now, I was even more curious to know what was behind that work of an old piece of art, that stood like a portal between two dimensions, I was also concerned with Gertrude.

What was wrong with her?

I just asked a simple question, but she has been acting weird since we left that one store for her "special" products. I don't know - but I will find out, I'm like the FBI on the Taliban, I get things done!

As I continued up the stairs, I heard a noise and looked back at the door for a second glance... smoke, and a purplish light, coming from beneath it.

"Oh, now that's strange," I whispered to myself, and my eyes bulged.

I headed back down the stairs to be nosy, while curiosity was running through my thick skull. Walking toward the door, slowly, and impatiently awaiting the approach, the floors began to creak, and I felt mild anxiety run up my spine.

Finally, arriving at the door, reaching my shaking hand to turn the doorknob. With so much anticipation flowing through my body, my heart pumps with such desire. When I was startled by a heavy voice, swinging around with the chills, it said with a low grainy mopey voice, "You should not... be….here".

It was Patrick.

"Geez," I squeezed my eyes in frustration, "Pat, you scared the crap out of me," I nervously said while still trying to catch the breath that seems to leave my body.

"I'm sorry…. Ms. Garcia, but you should get along now," with sorrow in his deep voice.

Huffing out of my nose, "Good night, Patrick," as I slogged away wretched.

Dragging my body back up the stairs once again for the millionth time, it seemed. I was even more intrusive with my tampering mind, as to what was behind that door that I wasn't even allowed to be by, it was killing me to find out.

Walking through my bedroom door, I felt frigid. Still pondering in my head about this town, the secrets, Patrick and Gertrude. My investigative strike has kicked in. While I was gazing around the room trying to figure if it could give some clues at all,

I started thinking, "Where the hell is the closet at?"

Finally, looking close enough, I noticed some hinges hanging out the sides behind my dresser.

"Huh, why would they want to hide the closet from me," I proclaimed to myself.

Moving my dresser out of the way, trying not to make too much noise. I finally got to the door. Tugging on the door was like a workout at the gym. It was stuck!

"Probably haven't been opened in decades," I was laughing at my sense of humor. A good 5 minutes later, I'm flying backward, hitting my head on my vanity, which I buffoonery placed behind me. Putting aside that I might now have a concussion. I stood up, in a bit of a daze.

Walking into the closet, trying to find a light, was only the easy part. Reaching for the cord, I tug on it, a light comes flickering on. Cobwebs filled the space, along with dust. Tons of boxes filled the shelves, but one box caught my attention the most. For one, it was pink, and I had not seen anything pink in Gertrude's house. Second, my mother's name, *Valentina Galva*, was written in black marker, decorated with glitter and stickers on the box. I hurried and snatched the box so quickly off the shelf; glitter and stickers came flying off like confetti. With my heart pounding faster than I could count, I opened the box, finding letters.....
tons and tons of letters, from my mother to Gertrude.

Opening up the first one slowly, wanting to preserve the delicate envelope the letter came in. The letter read:

"Dear Gerty,

I miss you so much; I do not know how to deal with this. I am all alone with this secret and have no one to share it with but you. Sometimes, I wish I were normal. Have a normal life and raise normal kids. When I get married, I plan on marrying a normal guy, so we can have semi-normal kids. Sorry, Gerty, I know this may hurt you, but this is how I feel, I will always love you, you are my sister, and that will never change, just accept what I want".

Sincerely Valentina"

"What the hell is she talking about," I interrogated my mind, and my stomach was in knots.

I continued to read more. Opening another with just as much caution as the previous one, this one was about me! It read:

"Dear Gerty,

*I tried everything I could from preventing this from happening, but it did anyway. She will be three on the 28th, and she is starting to move her toys in the air. I tried everything to keep it from her father, but he is starting to feel weird things around here. I tell him it's nothing; however, he continues to insist we should call the local pastor to come to the house. How do I tell him, no! Yeah, right, a pastor, my feet would begin to burn. I don't want her to be this; I'm doing **enlever ses pouvoirs** casting on her before the 28th. I have made my final decision, then when the time is right (if ever), I will give them back to her……."*

At this point in the letter, I cannot help but cringe with fear and nervousness on what the hell is going on here, I kept reading:

"….but I want her to have a normal childhood, and die naturally not with magic. I'm sorry to break this to you, Gerty, but I do not want my kids to be around you. Forgive me for this unfortunate

*surprise, and I do not want them to see what **YOU** are. Yes, I said*

"you" because I will live my life like an average human and not

a Witch..."

Sincerely Valentina

P.S. I will always love you"

Dropping the letter, as I quickly stood up. Everything seemed to be going in slow motion, time stopped, and vertigo shot through my body. I could not believe what I had just read. Was that for real, were my eyes playing a trick on me!

"Witches!" I exclaimed to myself, "Witches are not real," breathing heavily out my mouth, as I tried to keep my composure, I felt like I just ran a 5k in the dead of winter. Trying to comprehend the details of those letters.

This was a joke....a joke, right?

My hands were shaking, and I got really still. Not knowing what to do next, I just sat on my bed, with a blank, pale, stare while I looked into nowhere. Suddenly a knock on the door woke me out of my trance, I rushed to toss all the letters back in the box. Sliding the box under my bed,

"Come in," I said with a frog in my throat.

It was Gertrude

"Are you alright dear," Gertrude fixed her eyes at me, "I have been hearing some rumbling around up here for the past half hour, thought I'd come and check on...."

Stopping herself mid-sentence, her face went shallow, as she stared at my dresser. I forgot to move back into place, how stupid of me.

"Sandy?" She whispered as she approached my seemingly frail body.

Interrupting her

"I found them, Gertrude," I stammered with my words.

"Come with me.....," she sighed with delight in her voice, as she turns towards the door to walk away. I couldn't get my body to move, it was frozen like it was kept in this tomb of a room. My mind was in 5 different directions, try to figure out where to go.

"Sandy?" she pops her head back in the room,

"Come, dear."

My body seemed to float up and to the door, as I glided about the floors. Following her down the hallway, still in shock without a word to say about those letters, even though I had so much to declaim. Seemingly, sliding down the stairs, past the pictures, past the cats, she came to a halt at *the door,* that I was so jittery about. Turning around toward me she said,

"Are you ready?"

"Ready for what?" I questioned, still in shock.

"To change your whole life....," she said with excitement.

I gulped without saying a word.

She proceeded to open this heavy, ancient door that my mind had been crazy for.

As she opened the door, there seemed to be a dash of light and a hint of sage in the air....it was a whole new world as a bat flew past me, and I flinched, and Gertrude laughed. Cats, and

cauldrons; Bats hanging from the planked ceiling, and tarantulas;

walls filled with shelves, and on those shelves were tons of jars.

She had snakes and eyeballs, fingers, and frogs. I had to hold my

guts because I never saw anything like this in my life.

My face went pale with fright, Gertrude questions me.

"Are you okay?"

Still kind of freaked out, I responded, "Um, maybe."

I continued to follow her around as she continued to show the

disgusting things she was hiding. We arrived at a round table

with a five-pointed pentagram and sat; we then began to discuss

the letters:

"Witch?" was the only word I could get out of my mouth, I

nervously asked.

"Yes," we locked eyes are she responded, "Both of you are my

dear, your mother just wanted to live the life of a mortal," she

began to explain in detail, "We were blessed with this wonderful

gift, why would anyone want to live a normal life, is beyond me."

"Can I do some magic or no?" I began to lighten up to the idea.

"No, not really," she said without hesitation, "however, I can give you back your full powers; if you would like them?"

"Why, what happened to them?" I asked with such inquiring.

"It's because when you were a little girl your mother did the *enlever ses pouvoirs* on you, meaning, she took away your powers, so that you may live a normal life….," She continued, "and since you are getting older it may be harder to give them back…," she began to finish up, "However my dear, I know how to do the reversal…," she snickered at me with honor.

"Will it hurt? I mean, what will happen to me?".

"It might hurt…just for a bit…," she tried to persuade me.

"But my dear, you are a Galva, we are some of the strongest, wisest, loveliest, and sought after witches….in the world," she explained with pride, "and a Galva witch always has her powers, deep down inside of her."

Interrupting her exciting story,

"I think I know what you mean!" I rose up from the marvelous crafted chair, "When my friend was in the hospital, I went to go touch her hand, and I shocked her …I mean, like, really hard. Not just a little static shock," I enthusiastically said, "but a white light came out of my hand, and she woke up. I was so scared that day, I didn't know what to think."

"Yes, my darling, they're coming back," she smiled, thrilled. Killing her smile with my next question,

"but what do you mean that a Galva witch is the most sought after?" I question because that intrigued my mind.

"My dear, a Galva witch is the best of the best, it is hard for us to die. We can do 99% of all magic, and other witches, warlocks and wizards can only do about 80%, and they envy that…," She discussed, "And so for a Galva witch to pass, her body must be cremated and made into a brew and drunken under an eclipsed moon, but…," She began to finish, "to cremate us, they must first remove the heart from our body with a special dagger, called the

Falker Dagger, which can penetrate a Galva's bodies, to get to our heart."

"This is why we are also seen as a threat to all *others*," she continued.

"Where is the Falker dagger?" I got closer with excitement.

Gertrude smiles and puts a finger up to her lips, "shhh."

Taking everything in, the look on my face was a look of fascination that I am part of such a prestigious group of witches; I couldn't wait to begin my new journey, I felt more calm coming into this town and now - I know why. This was my calling, I'm finally able to see everything so much clearer.

"Ok, then, can we get this casting going, I want to learn everything!" I exclaimed while clapping my hands.

Gertrude laughed, "Ok, let's get ready; however, getting your powers back is not as simple as taking them away," she explained, "It could cause …...discomfort, and you may be unable to control them."

"Then we better start now, so by the time school starts, the sparks don't go flying off anywhere," I joked.

"You plan on going to a public school? With those disgusting, worthless fickles?" She asked with disgust.

"Fickles?" my eyebrows went up.

"Yes, fickles - humans, in the witchy world, they are called fickles; a person without interest or loyalty. That is what they are, fickles are self-absorbed sponges with no sense of stability, they are unpredictable and moody.

"Hey, I'm half-fickle too ok and yeah, why not?", I stood there with a hand on my hip,

"I need to meet some people, get out, and start a new life outside of Little Falls," I replied with vexation.

"I guess then," Gertrude sighed, with annoyance, " Don't say I didn't warn you if the fickles come for you, my dear, but if they do," Gertrude chuckled with self-assurance," we'll be ready but ok - shall we get started!"

Chapter

8

A New Start

First-day training went......well...... somewhat weird, I

needed to get the spell that my mother cast on me....off. Gertrude

had made a *brew*, which had roaches, spiders, and other nasty

looking things in it! I wasn't sure what she wanted me to do with

it, but there was no way in hot hell balls; I was going to drink this

- um nope, not me. As I walked into *"the room,"* the smell was so

overwhelming, I couldn't help but gag.

"Smells delish, huh?" Gertrude smiled.

"Not quite my cup of tea," I disgustingly responded to her

question.

 "Well, let's begin, have a seat, my dear," as she ushered my

edgy body.

"Sit!"

I sat in this seat that had straps at the wrist and ankles. At first, I

was excited for this to begin, but now I'm kind of having second thoughts. As I began to sit down, I just felt this overwhelming sensation hit my body like a cool breeze.

"Just relax; it will be over sooner than you know it," Gertrude reassured me.

"Um, Gerty, are you using these straps on me?" I nervously asked as I sat down in this horrid chair, that scared me.

"Uh…yes…yes, my darling," She hesitated to answer.

"What!" I jumped up and screamed, "Noooo."

"It will only be uncomfortable, but only for a few minutes," Gertrude scrambled to calm me down.

"Oh my god,…oh…my…god…what did I get myself into!" I raised my voice with a squeal.

Gertrude proceeded to push my hesitant body into the chair and began applying the strap restraint to both my wrist and ankles.

"Now," Gertrude tries to release my anticipated mind," just relax, my darling, this will be quick."

She began…..

"Royaume divin, retourne-lui ce qui lui a été enlevé, refais-lui la vie à la façon Galva!"

Divine Realm, return to her what was taken away, make her whole again the Galva way

I started to twitch, and it felt like thousands of bolts of lightning were going through my body; it was so unbearable, I nearly passed out. A blast of greenish-purple mist shot up through the chimney and into the sky. After a few moments, the fog then retracted back into my body, like a slug curling up from salt, knocking my chair over, hitting my head so hard I got knocked out.

Waking up to Patrick and Gertrude standing over my body, "quite a bump," Gertrude says, with a smirk on her face; as she helps me up.

"What happened?" I question as I try to sit up and get dizzy at that attempt.

"Rest my dear, just rest," as Gertrude lays a hand on my shoulder to relax my relentless body,

"You need your strength for training, and you start school on Monday, and I wouldn't want you to be too worked up."

I couldn't rest, I couldn't relax….I wanted to practice my magic. As I lay there on the couch, "Ok, I'll just lay right here," I reassured Gertrude.

"All right dear, I'm going into my office, call Patrick or me if you need anything."

"Okay," I whispered as I got back comfortable on the couch …..with a plan in mind.

Once Gertrude turned away, and I saw Patrick disappear into the house….I sat up.

"If you won't teach me now, I'll have to teach myself," I mischievously smirked to my unknowing mind. "Now, what can I practice on," I whisper to myself, as I glance around at the crowded living room.

Sitting across the room was one of many cats Gertrude had. What a perfect practice subject or so I thought.

"Ok, Sandy," I crazily said to myself, "what do you remember from the movies? A wiggle from the nose, a wand, or a simple finger point might do?" I embarrassedly tried to remember all the 'witch' movies I had seen throughout my miserable, pathetic fickle life.

Well, I couldn't wiggle my nose, and I had no wand, so I guess my finger would have to do. As I stared at the cat, thinking about what I could possibly turn it into.

"Ooooooh a dog....I'll turn you into a dog," I was talking to the cat who seemed to linger to every word I said, "Stay still ok," I told it like it understands what I meant.

"Ok, so in the movies, they say whatever comes to mind," I stretch my hands out, palms forwards, and crack my knuckles. Closing my eyes and pointing my finger at the cat.

"Kitty cat so dark, sitting in the light, be a cat by day and dog by night,"

Opening 1 eye, then both eyes to a confused cat staring at my finger and then licks it.

"Guess, that didn't work," I wondered discouraged as I laid back down, staring at the cat for a minute more as it jumped off the end table.

I was trying to figure out what might have gone wrong.

"Ah well ….let me rest up," closing my eyes once again to see what the next few days hold for me.

Well, today is the first day of school, and I'm feeling great. New shoes, new clothes, hair did just right. Staring in the mirror as I admire my 'new' Sandy.

"This is as good as it gets," I joked to my reflection in the mirror, wearing a pair of high waisted ripped jeans and a pink cropped top that tied right where my pants met it and brown leather boots.

"Sandy, my dear, it's late for your fickles," Gertrude calls for me at the front door.

Her and fickles - I laughed

"Coming, as I run out my bedroom door, grabbing my new silver sequined backpack. Hurrying down the stairs, I trip over Jasper.

"Ugh cat, move," I urged to his nonchalant attitude, he was still trying to glare through my soul as I hurried past.

Hopping over the last few steps of the staircase

"Let's go," I smiled at Gertrude.

"Food?" She asked as she pointed to the kitchen.

"No, I'm abnormally nervous I can't eat," I gushed and my stomach started turning in knots.

"Well, take an apple just in case," She pushed.

"Fine," holding out my hands as she tossed it to me.

Finally walking out the door, I turn to Gertrude

"What's wrong, aren't you taking me," I questioned.

"No, my dear," She responded, "Patrick will take you."

"In the old limo! No, thank you," I pressed, I'll walk.

"No…just take the Mercedes then," She insisted.

"Awesome!" I was hoping she would give me the pleasure of riding around in this beautiful machinery.

She dangled the keys by her perfectly shaped ears, I ran and grabbed them; running so fast to the Mercedes, I forgot to give Gertrude a hug. Hopping in the car and rolling down the window "BYE!"

Gertrude was waving at me as I was driving out the driveway, onto a new world and a new sense of being. My stomach was in knots the whole way.

As I was pulling up to the school with a sense of freshness and excitement, hoping to run into Cole, whom I hadn't seen in weeks since I saw him walking down the street. Scoping out a place to park, I finally see an open space. I swerve the Benz in the tightly placed markers, stepping onto my new school grounds was a bit refreshing, as I look around and see the car next to me; slowly begins to open the door.

"Sandy?" a soft voice calls.

It was Cole…..My heart stopped!

"Oh my god, hi," as I walked over, trying not to embarrass my life, "I guess you found me," I laughed.

'Yeah, I guess I did" He stammered while staring into my eyes with a smile on his face, "I'll walk you inside if you like."

"Ok," I agreed with my flirty smile, and our shoulders touching. I felt like I was flying.

Until….

"Cole!" a chilled, nasal voice calls.

Allowing my eyes to follow the nauseous voice, I see a girl with shoulder-length brown hair with overdone highlights, a little taller than I, and a bit thicker in the hips.

"I've missed you," she said to Cole while ignoring my presence.

"June…," Cole begins, "We're done, I told you that at the start of summer."

I thought to myself, "Time to go."

"Um, I'll catch you later, Cole, I need to figure my way around," I crookedly smiled at him and her, and I hurried away as fast I could.

"Sandy, wait….," Cole called out to me, and I had to ignore him.

"Ugh, how stupid can I be to believe a guy as cute and popular as Cole, would be single," I ran over this thought in my head, until I reach my homeroom for 1st period.

Still kind of dumbfounded, as I walked in late to everyone staring at me, I quickly found a seat, still thinking about Cole....just at that moment he came scurrying into the room.

"Sorry, *teach*," He apologizes, as he makes his way into the room, we then lock eyes as he notices that we were in the same class together. He approached the empty desk next to me.

"Sorry, about June," He whispers, "She's my ex."

"It's fine," I reassured him, "There is nothing to apologize about," as I glanced at his beautiful face.

I had to turn away and quick.

"Quite," the teacher exclaims, as he looks over his black-rimmed glasses. I chuckle and raise my finger to my mouth, "Shhhhh," I tell Cole. Who then mocks my movement and turns forward. We both seamlessly smiled together in perfect harmony.

After the first period, Cole had grabbed me in the hall, by my hand.

"Hey, can we talk?" He asks.

"Sure, about what?" as I lean against the grey hall lockers.

"At the beginning of each year, we have a bonfire in Mr. McGregor's cornfield," He hesitated, "…and I was wondering if you would like to come with me?"

Blushing uncontrollably, "Of course, that sounds super fun," I gushed, and we exchanged phone numbers.

"Cool, so I'll text you all the details, and….it's a date," He blurted.

"It's a date," I gushed back.

"I'll see you around, yeah, got to get going," He explains.

"Bye," I waved as he walked away. My stomach turned with delight, and I was in yet another fantasy daze until I lost my balance, and I dropped my books; they all fell to the dirty checkered floor.

"Uh, excuse you," a snotty voice says.

It was June.

"Watch it, new girl," she snarls, "Cole is taken, you hear me,"
rolling her eyes as she walks away.

"Oh god, not another Danijela," my mind raced.

"Oh, this is going to be SUPER," I say to myself, expecting
another plastic Barbie.

Going through the rest of the day seemed to drag on, but I was ok
with it. I felt alive! Everything seemed to be falling into place as
it should.

Ending my first day of school, as the bell rang, and I headed to
the parking lot.

"Hey, Sandy," I heard a familiar voice call me from behind.

I turned around in blissful delight.

"Hey, Cole," I turned red, and tuck my hair behind my ear.

"I was thinking," he began, with his hands in his pockets, "If
maybe....you wanted to go over our syllabus for class?" He asks.

I look at the ground and chuckle, "That would be great actually,"

I didn't even hesitate to invite him over, "You can follow me

back to my house?"

"Yeah, let's go," He got excited and hopped in his car.

I then hopped in and took off, with him following close behind, I

heart couldn't stop pounding. I couldn't stop looking in the

rearview mirror to make sure he hasn't abandoned the venture.

Arriving at Gertrude's fortress, I parked the car and was

followed by Cole, who trailed close behind.

"This is your place, huh?" he curiously inquired.

"Yeah, I stay with my Aunt….pretty cool, huh!"

"Yeah - cool," he takes off his sunglasses in a playful manner.

"Come on, let's go inside," I pushed without hesitation.

Walking in through the doors, I felt anxious.

"Welcome to my abode," I joked.

"Why, thank you, my lady," he played back.

"Sandy?" Gertrude calls as she walks from the back, halting as

she sees Cole standing there.

"Why...hello," Gertrude bashfully holds out her hand

"Gerty, this is Cole."

"Cole, my aunt Gerty," I introduce them both

"Nice, to meet you," Cole says as he takes Gertrude's hand.

"I invited him over I hope that's okay," I asked without hesitation and hoped she didn't mind, "we're going to go over our syllabus, we are in the same homeroom together," I blurted out random facts.

"He was nice enough to come over and help me with the syllabus," giving Gertrude the *eyes*.

"Of course it is darling, would you guys like something to eat or drink," Gertrude offers as she stares at us with a bit of a mysterious smirk on her face.

I sense that something is off.

"I'll have water," Cole responds immediately.

"Uh me too," as I stare at the smile on Cole's face.

"Ok, will be right back," Gertrude faintly says as she goes into the kitchen to grab water.

Cole and I relax on the couch, as we sink deeper in, we look at each other.

Catching that I am holding onto this glance a little longer than I should, "Um yeah, so let's begin," I fumbled to get my words out.

"Here we are," Gertrude interrupts the awkward tension, setting both glasses on the coffee table.

"I'll be in the back if you need me," She continues, "Sandy......," I look up at her, "if you need anything just let me know," she smiles as she takes off into the back.

As we went over the syllabus, I couldn't help but notice how beautiful Cole was just sitting there. I didn't even realize that my body automatically got closer to his. Feeling my vibrations get close to him as I was taking in everything he was me telling me, putting all my being into his words, that my endless thoughts were lingering on to the lasting breaths he was taking after every exhale. At this point, the syllabus was so far out of my mind; I don't even remember the first sentence.

Interrupting him, "would you like to see my room?" I bashfully divulge my thoughts, wondering if he'd accept my offer.

"Don't worry about all the cats, they're very friendly," I began an irrelevant conversation to keep it from getting too heavy, "Except for Jasper but you'll know it's home when you come across."

He chuckles, omg my heart melts, his laugh I could just fall in love.

Turning around to break my trance, "Follow me."

We set our books down, and I led him on a tour of the crazy abode I lived in, walking down the hallways, he seemed to get overwhelmed, and he looked a bit off. I turned, "Are you okay, Cole?"

He hesitated to answer me, "Yeah - I'm fine, but I think I should get going."

"Okay," A little disappointed that he wanted to leave so soon but understanding. Maybe, it was best if he left, possibly -if he saw something in this house and started freaking out, that would cause problems, right? Perhaps he saw something, and that's why he's freaked out and wants to leave. So many thoughts clouded

my mind while walking him back to the front door.

"I'm sorry," he says while staring at me with his fixed eyes.

"No, worries," we'll see each other soon, I reassured him.

Opening the door for him.

"I'll see you later, Sandy," he says while giving me one last

glare, as he leans in to kiss my cheek, "You know, Sandy I really

like you, and I feel you will fit in very well here."

Walking away, I watched like a creeper, as he got into his car

and just the thought of his soft, warm lips lingering on my cheek

I can only imagine what it feels like to kiss on the lips, waving

goodbye. I slowly close the door.

Chapter

9

Timing

A few weeks have gone by, and Cole and I have gotten even closer. We spend every moment we can with each other. We have been inseparable. I have taken a very keen liking to him; he is everything I could want. Tonight is the bonfire, and I was more excited than ever to be by him once again

"I'm headed out Gerty," As I yell, making my way to the front door.

"Have fun my darling, I'm a call away and behave yourself," she smiles at me

I smile back and run out the door. Arriving at Mr. McGregor's cornfield bonfire, I show up to this crowded mess of adventure, full of kids from school and a lot of new faces, tons of music, and just everyone having fun. I spot in the distance Cole sitting there with his friends, only at that moment he turns around, and we lock eyes, he leaves his buddy in mid-sentence to come and greet me, "Hi, Sandy," he leans in for one of his fantastic cheek kisses, "I've been waiting for you!" He gets excited and grabs my hand

"Well, I'm here," I smile, "So, what do we do?" I question as everyone was just relaxing and having fun.

"Anything you want," he walks me through the crowd.

"I feel like there's going to be like one of those murder scenes off of movies, and someone is just going to come with the machete and chop everyone up," I blabbed my horrific horror movie fanatic stories. Cole's face is in dismay, and then he laughs, "My kind of girl."

"I love horror movies, I'm not just a pretty face," I shrug my shoulder up and smile.

"No, you're not - you're beautiful," Cole says to me while moving the stray hairs from my face.

I look away, I couldn't keep eye contact with him any longer.

"Hey, let me introduce you to some of the guys," he says as we begin walking over to a group.

"Guys - Sandy….Sandy - Guys," Cole points and makes a marvelous introduction.

Everyone waves and says hi and Cole and I find a spot to sit, as we talk the night away, my heart begins to pump faster, and my stomach goes in many knots. I can't stop smiling, I can't control my grin. I don't want to either.

"COLE!" the ambiance gets interrupted. It was June.

"Are we still going to Prom?" she stands with her hand on her hip, completely ignoring the fact, I was sitting there.

"June….really?" Cole is annoyed, "We broke up, and I'm seeing someone else now."

My mind couldn't grasp what he just said, he was seeing someone else…. me?

"WHAT!" June exclaims while trying to cause a crowd of attention, "HER….you promised me we'd go to prom no matter what, so you break promises now Cole," June annoyingly picks at Cole's emotions.

"Just leave June, there is no reason for this, Sandy is my new girlfriend, I'm not going to prom with you, her and I are going."

"We are?" I thought to myself, feeling very much taken back in a good way.

"UGH," June screams as she stomps away.

"I'm so sorry, Sandy," Cole grabs me.

"So….," a smile breaks my face, "I'm your new girlfriend?"

"If you'd do me the honor?" Cole smiles.

I nod my head in assurance

He reaches in and grabs my face, I begin to prepare my mind and body, this is what I had been waiting for since the first time I laid my eyes on him.

He leans in and kisses me, this was more than I expected and MORE. I was on Cloud 9 and couldn't have been happier. I never thought I'd have these kinds of feelings for anyone. I was more than happy, pulling back, we just stared in each other's eyes and lost track of time. It felt like time stood still. There was no care in the world, but he and I and I wanted this to last. He pointed to the sky, at a star shining the brightest, "That star is for you, I'll call it 'Sandygalactic," we both laughed at the name, "Now, that you're up there, all the other stars can disappear and die because none of them can EVER shine brighter than you," I get lost in his words, as he holds me tighter. I feel at home.

A few weeks after the bonfire and Cole has been the most romantic; he has brought me flowers every day; he has been there when I needed him the most without hesitation, and make sure I'm not without and his poems…..oh god, I'm in love with his poetry, he has written me at least 20 of his magical pieces of artwork. He even made a book for me, and bought me my favorite chocolate with almonds, I'm so infatuated with this guy! I'm looking forward to seeing what the future has in store for us.

"Want to come over after school?" I stop Cole in the hallway between classes.

"Of course," he kisses my cheek, "meet you out front," he pokes my cheek as he dashes down the hallway.

With Cole following close behind after school, we arrive back at Gertrude's. Meeting each other by the front of my car, Cole grabs my hand, "It is ok if I hold your hand?"

"I don't see a problem, you are my boyfriend now," my overly girly emotions were taking over, and I couldn't help but keep my eyes on him.

However, as we approached the front door, I felt my heart drop, and I felt overly eager. Opening the door, holding hands with Cole.

"AHHHHHHHHHHHHH," a hurl of screams knocked me back. Immediately dropping Cole's hand.

Cole, Gertrude, Patrick, and the cat all cringe with pain from the squealing piglets that filled the living room.

"Julie,.... Fayth, ...Alex!"

We all let out another horrid nail-biting screech as we run to each other with open arms and tears in their eyes.

"How.... What......," I contemplate.

"Your Aunt Gertrude," Julie says as she looks at Gertrude.

"What!" I exclaim with excitement. "I just can't believe you girls are here with me.....for how long?"

"Just a few days," Fayth reassures.

"Well…..," Alex says while nudging my exhausted body and clearing up her fabricated sore throat, "Who is this?".

"Oh, I'm sorry," looking back at Cole, "This is Cole, my boyfriend."

"Nice to meet you, ladies," Cole says with a smile on his face, making them all fall for him.

"Hi," they all fumble to get the first *"hi"* out.

"Hey Sandy, I'm just going to go, you have a lot to catch up on," he insists on exiting the slumber party.

"Ok, text me."

They couldn't even wait until he was all the way out of the door.

"Wow! he is gorgeous!" all the girls gush and squeal.

"I know, isn't he, he is the only one that will keep me sane while I'm here in Salem," I explain.

"But enough about him, what do you ladies have to do, you guys are only here for a few days, so let's make it count!" I hurried the subject, afraid that there will not be enough time to catch up,

"There isn't much to do in Salem, but I can take you to this burger place, and we can talk."

"Yum," Fayth hums, "I'm starving!"

"Gerty, we will be back," I call out.

"Ok, sweetie, don't be back too late," she agreed.

Arriving at Burger Palace, we find a seat at a booth. Waiting to catch up on lost time between us all.

"So, I guess KY isn't doing that good," Julie confesses

"Why?" My heartfelt mind questioned with sadness.

"He is acting really weird, and doesn't want to hang out with anyone anymore," Julie explains.

"Yeah, From what I heard," Alex interrupts, "He is really down about not being able to see you or talk to you before you left."

"Well, that is his fault; he hasn't written to me or called me since I have been here, but I don't want to think about him. I have Cole now, and he is more than enough for me," telling the girls, trying to convince them that I haven't been thinking about Ky since I got here, which was a lie.

A thick silence filled the table as the conversation felt awkward, and we were unsure of what to say. Was I falling for KY more than I wanted to just by hearing of how sad and hurt he was, or was I feeling bad for him because I didn't let our friendship turn into something more? Breaking the silence, Julie says,

"Well, musketeers, I feel fat enough; let us head back to your mansion and get ready for our sleepover.

"Let's go!" Alex abruptly shouts more than she needed to, but that is just Alex's fashion.

Driving back to Gertrude's felt like an eternity because all that was rushing through my mind was KY. Why was I feeling like this, I didn't want him in my head...... I daze off daydreaming about KY and a "what if" situation? What if he calls me, what if he comes out here to see, what if....?

"SANDY, look out!" Julie shouts.

I slam on the breaks, headlights beaming, and dust particles flying in the air, a baby deer standing there waiting for its mother on the other side. Oh god, I feel like this family curse will never end. I slowly thought in my head.

"Are you ok, Sandy?" Fayth asks with caution.

"Yeah...., yeah, I'm fine," I reassured them.

They all looked at me like I was a totally changed girl and Salem was changing me, I realized I'm not the same girl; I was a few months ago; I think I'm just...growing into a young.....and I hesitated to even consider this thought but a witch.....

Getting back at Gertrude's house was a sigh of relief for the girls who felt their lives could have ended tonight because of my selfish daydreaming, but I could never let them know that I think I was falling for KY, what would they think? What would they say? Would they tell KY? Or worse, what if Cole found out. I think this is something I would have to keep for myself, keep those persistent pounding thoughts in my secret mental stash. Watching the girls walk in front of me felt…..awkward; I don't know why.

Looking back at me with curiosity, Julie yells out to me, "hurry up, slowpoke."

And a smile breaks across my face as I hurry to follow them through the front doors.

Gertrude sitting deep on her sofa reading a book.

"How did it go ladies, did you girls catch up on a lot," Gertrude insisted on all the juicy gossip.

"It went very well, we caught up on all our missed time together, but now we are going to go to sleep.

"Of course, my dear," Gertrude says as she looks deep into my soul, knowing there was something wrong.

Leading the girls up to my room, they are admiring all the "artwork" Gertrude has.

"Wow, all this stuff looks so ….ancient," Fayth says, wiping her finger across the dusted filled walls.

"I know Gertrude is somewhat of a collector, I guess you could say," responding but not trying to give much away.

Arriving in my bedroom door, the girls didn't even wait for me to open it; they let themselves in with more force than I could handle.

"Oh nice room Sandy, you are living the life," Alex reminds me, "this house is awesome, your aunt is awesome, and this room is wicked awesome," as she begins her own personal tour of my room décor.

"I'm glad you girls are here," I tear up, "It has been pretty lonely here, and Cole is my only real friend, I mean of course I'll make more friends, and I've befriended a few girls at school, but they are nothing compared to you three.

"Awwww," they all say in sync with one another.

"So, tell us more about Cole?" his name seemed to roll off Julie's tongue as she said her words with strength, "Well I met him at Burger Palace one day, and we just seem to click," I took a deep breath as KY flashed through my mind and I chuckled.

"He is so gorgeous, and we got to know each better when we met up again at a bonfire in one of the many cornfields here.

The girl's smiles seem to break their cheeks as they all blushed and gush over the story I was telling them.

"He is everything that I needed to be more comfortable here; he makes me smile and laugh at all his silly little jokes. I can't say I love him, but I do very much like him a lot," I seamlessly protruded my throbbing mind.

"You guys look so cute together," Fayth gushes as she seems to daydream about being Mrs. Cole Creek, "He is extra sexy."

"Extra sexy," Julie laughs, "I never knew there was such a thing."

We all laugh and poke fun at Fayth and at her extra sexy comment.

"He's mine, ok," I giggled at Fayth, knowing she meant no harm.

"Well, Sandy.....," Julie begins with a grin, "How do you truly feel about KY?"

All the girls close in, trying to peep my thoughts before I could say a word.

I couldn't hold back anymore, and I had to tell them what I was thinking,

"I think, I have feelings for KY, and it is causing confusion now because I'm with cole," I spilled all my secrets, my waterfall of a mouth just blurted it all out, and now I could only pray that these girls would keep this secret.

All their eyes seem to be amazed but yet confused and concerned in some way.

"Don't tell a soul," I threatened them all with my words, "I'll kill every one of you, slowly," I joked.

"Cross our hearts, Sandy," they reassured me.

However, with this kind of secret, I'm not sure Jules or Alex could keep. I feared the worst was coming, only time would tell the ending to this story.

Laying down we all just seemed to drift into a deep sleep, and in the morning, I woke up to an empty bedroom and something.......different, a different smell was brewing in the kitchen

As I scurry downstairs, there were all 3 girls and Gertrude in the kitchen.....cooking.....food. Not just any food.... typical food–I thought.

"Oh my god, it smells good!" I commented, as the smell of eggs, bacon, and toast filled the thick air. A familiar scent that I was not used to since living with Gertrude but a familiar smell from my childhood that brought back memories from beyond the grave.

As we sat around the breakfast table laughing and talking while Jasper was nearby scratching at the stove, trying to figure out was this unusual smell. I looked at each of my friends and thanked myself for keeping them in my life and turning to make sure I acknowledge Gertrude for taking me into her house from a sister who didn't want her to know me. I felt like this is where I belonged. This is where I'm supposed to be, and I'm happy.

"Ok, girls," Gertrude interrupts the laughs that filled the area, "We need to get going to the airport," Gertrude stood up from the table and picked up our plates, "we don't want to keep your moms waiting for much longer."

"Do they have to?" I chuckled as I hugged Julie, who was placed stuck to my arm, "couldn't they live with us.....for like.....ever," I amused them all with my joyous sentences as their faces light up.

"I wish!" Alex said as she put her arm around me, "but you know it won't hurt for you to come and visit us sometimes either."

"I know, I will make time," I reassured her and then hugged her tightly, "I promise."

"Patrick," Gertrude called out, "place these lovely ladies' suitcase in the car."

"At your command, my lady," Patrick obeyed with his moped response.

Heading to the airport, I watched them laugh and cry and laugh more. My other pieces of sanity, leaving me. Everything was in slow motions, and I wasn't ready for them to go, I felt a bit lost knowing I wouldn't see them for a while. Arriving at the airport felt all too familiar, when they were the ones dropping ME off when I was leaving Little Falls, I didn't want to feel like this again, but I was; I felt overwhelmed and sad. Waving bye to them was the hardest thing since leaving home the first time. Now, I would have to suffer over again.

Chapter

10

So it begins

At school, on Monday, we began studying the Salem witch trials, a topic I seemed to be most interested in, and as the new girl in school, it was hard for me to find kind friends to help study. Still, I did seem to make a new enemy pretty easy, especially with June. June has short brown hair with too big, overdone highlights that surround her face in all the wrong areas, she is Cole's ex but not wanting to comprehend that. It is very noticeable that she still wants to be with Cole and wants me out of the picture. Now, she doesn't seem like Cole's type, and I think that is why she is always giving me nasty looks; I don't know what to do, other than ignoring her and continuing my relationship with Cole, she is not essential in my life, so I will show her no importance.

"Hey babe," Cole says, coming from behind me with a single white rose with a teddy bear hanging on to it.

"Oh, how cute, thanks, baby," as I hugged him, noticing June in the background giving Cole and me a smirk evil grin.

"There is your other girlfriend," I joke with him.

"Please, she is nowhere near as perfect as you," He tells me while tapping the tip of my nose with his index finger.

"But I didn't come here to talk about her, I wanted to say congratulations on the prom court.

"What!" I exclaimed, "What do you mean?"

"Yeah, they announced it 1st period," he looked at me like I knew this.

"Oh, I was late to school, I just got here," I told him with a shocked face.

"Who would nominate me, I don't really talk to many people."

"Well, you are the new face of Salem High School, baby, so wear it proudly," Cole puts his arm around me as we walk to class.

Walking through the halls way, I felt an overwhelming sensation of the past. The last time I walked down a hallway and all eyes were on me, was the time my mother passed away. I don't know if I could handle this.

"I need to use the restroom," I rush away, leaving Cole standing solo, wondering what was wrong.

I ran to the bathroom, found a graffiti-filled stall, and slammed the door; I tried to stay in there as long as possible so that maybe the hallways would be clear from all the gossip when I exited. Waiting a few more moments, I poked my head out of the bathroom, meeting it with Coles.

"Are you ok?" He asked me with concern.

"Yeah, I -,," I begin, "I don't think that I'm ready for this," I abruptly answered him.

He laughs as I seem to overreact

"Sandy…. It is just prom queen nomination, not a Grammy, relax, everything will be fine," he touches my shoulder and brings my body towards him.

Later, on that day, I arrived home. And inform Gertrude on the good news.

"That is awesome my darling!" she seemed more excited than me for some reason, "So, I guess this means, we need to go dress shopping....yes?" Gertrude proceeds to question my roaming mind.

"Yes," I say shyly, with a small break of a smile.

Gertrude grabs the purse that always seems to be by her at all times.

"Let's go!" she hurries me out the door.

Leaving the house in a hurry, we headed out on this dress buying excursion. Headed into town was the least of my worries. I needed a dress that would announce my incredible presence here in Salem! I needed a WOW dress.

Going to at least 8 different stores, I finally picked out a gorgeous, turquoise half sequined gown that glittered in the sunlight that came shining through the window, and I felt like Cinderella.

All the ladies in the store seem to find their way over to me, to admire the gown, more than myself.

"Oh my word,…..that is stunning," the lady next to me utters.

"Thank you," I responded with such embarrassment. Not wanting to stand there and talk to her, I wasn't that sociable and a bit introverted, to strike up a conversation with a strange woman that was looking at me like a piece of meat, she saw on sale at the food market. As I headed back in the dressing room. Feeling like that paparazzi was following like a celebrity In this extravagant gown at the Oscars.

I hear Gertrude say, "I think that is the one, what do you think?"

"I think so," I said as I came out of the room, holding the dress with extreme caution, as not to let it drag on the ground. Walking up to the checkout counter, my stomach growls, and butterflies fill its capacity and get a feeling of nervousness and an overwhelming sensation.

"I'm hungry," I informed Gertrude, I needed to feed my body. I felt I could eat a cow, how I felt all the nerves running through my body were like a stream running through the mountains, and my blood felt as cold, and it was.

"What's wrong, my darling," Gertrude asks.

"I'm just - I wish my mom were here to see this," I held back my tears.

I explained to Gertrude all the beautiful things that my mom and I would do as I was growing up.

"What did you guys do growing up," I took the attention off of me.

"Oh, my darling!" Gertrude begins without hesitation, "we did so many unusual things, outrageous, mischievous outings, Val and I did.

"But my dear, you and your mother did so many things…..and I want you to finish," Gertrude starts, "And….I wouldn't mind, having a blast from the past on my many adventures my sister and I had."

Headed to the counter to pay, "That would be awesome, Gertrude! I'd like to see what my mother was like as a child."

Gertrude walks away from the counter after paying with a smile, and she turns, "Shall we?"

Smiling slightly and following Gerty on this unpredictable adventure that she had built in her mind. We took off on an adventure around Salem!

During our list of crazy rendezvous, we run into Cole and his friends.

"Hey babe," Cole approaches me and kisses me with his soft embrace.

Gertrude turning away awkwardly

"There is a house at Garrett's tonight, want to join us?" He asks me while looking over at Gertrude, hoping she was overhearing.

"Gerty," I turn to her.

"Yes, you may," As if she had been nosy the whole time

"Thank you, thank you!" I hug Gertrude and run off with Cole.

"Don't be back too late," She calls out to us

"I'll have her back at a reasonable hour," Cole calls back out to her, hoping to rest her mind.

Gertrude just standing there with a smirk, I felt a tad bit bad for leaving her, but I wanted to be by Cole, and hopefully, she understands.

Getting to Garrett's house, Cole grabs me and kisses me

"I can't stop kissing you, Sandy," Cole grabs my face, "I'm lost in you."

My hand rests against his, "I'm lost in you," I repeat as we go in for yet another embrace.

Coming up for air, we immediately begin dancing, getting lost in each other's presence. I swear, I feel like I'm flying, and I don't plan to come down anytime soon. Cole is my being, my peace, my soul. Watching him dance makes me fall for him even more than I had ever imagined. If I never knew love before, I think I know now. Keeping my eye glued to Cole while his hand seems to be attached to my hip. My train of thought gets interrupted when some guys come and try to crash the party.

"Hey man, get lost," Cole approaches the group without fear.

"Who are you?" the guy pokes Cole's chest.

"Well, I'm Cole - and this is an invitation-only party, and since it's my cousin's house," Cole starts," You….," Cole taps the guy's shoulder, "weren't invited."

"Please, man….," the guy is asking for trouble, "I do what I want," edging closer to Cole, "And when …..I want."

The whole party was now focused on this stirring feud.

"So, back off and don't make me mad," this stranger pushes Cole.

Without warning and in a blink of an eye, the guy was getting tossed across the room, and I mean like LITERALLY; Cole picked him up and threw him like a rag doll.

At this point, the entire party was in shock and awe.

Jumping in to defend their friend, the three goons that arrived with this boy all jumped Cole. I was getting more frightened and just wanted to leave, but in dismay, I couldn't believe what I was seeing. Cole was VISIBLY getting bulked up by the minute, by the hype of the circumstances. HE fights all three!!!

"COLE!" Garrett and a few other of his cousins pull him back," Let it go!"

Bursting from his cousin's grips, Cole takes off outside, I directly follow behind him.

"Cole?" I chase him and grab his shoulder.

Turning around without realization, "LEAVE ME BE!" he snaps at me in a scorn voice.

In disbelief, "Cole - you need to calm down, I'm here to help you, how dare you raise your voice at me like that!" I scorn him back

"Sandy - I'm…..," He begins with a pathetic apology.

"No….," get your thoughts together and text me when you do. I walk away, dumbfounded. Turning back around to finish my last parting words, "and don't think I'm going to go to prom with you…..I've dealt with enough," I start to giving Cole a piece of my mind, "If you are calmed by tomorrow be at my house by

6….if not, don't bother," I take off without another word and leave him there in his tracks.

Arriving back at Gertrude on foot, I stormed through the door and began my trek up the stairs.

"Sandy?" Gertrude announces, walking from the kitchen with a towel in her wet hands.

"Please, Gerty," I tear up, "I just want to go to bed."

As I make my way up to my room and throw myself on the bed.

A beautiful night turned into a disaster. I just wanted to sleep and forget this ever happened. Prom is tomorrow, I need some sleep to even begin to deal with that.

Waking up the following day, I felt sad. Cole and I just had our first fight and the day before prom nonetheless.

Gertrude pokes her head in my room, "It's time to get ready, dear." She announces.

Getting ready, I become emotional.

"What's wrong, my darling?" Gertrude turns me around.

"It's just - my mom.….," I hold back my tears, "She'd want to see this."

"I know Sandy," Gertrude tries to calm my mind, "But - she is always with you - always," she continues, "A witch's spirit doesn't disperse that easy my darling, we are the best in the world, this means, our souls live on," she finished putting the finishing touches on my hair.

Just as she finishes, there is a knock at the door.

I flip my head to the clock.…6 o'clock on the dot, I knew it was Cole.

As I make My way down the staircase, Cole sitting there with a giant bouquet of white roses with one black rose neatly tucked in the front, I approached him.

"Forgive me?" his eyes meet mine as he hands me the roses.

"Forgive you," I repeat, setting the Roses down.

"I brought your corsage.…," Cole announces as he takes out a beautifully decorated piece.

Finishing our pre-prom obligations, after Gertrude takes 101 pictures, we head out the door and in the limo.

Let the night begin.

Making our way through the doors, we got all the stares as we walked through the crowd, and the *'oohs and aaaa'* followed.

After a night of dancing, it was finally time to announce Prom Queen. Holding my breath....

"And the new Salem High School Prom queen is......"

Anticipation filled my anxious body, not knowing what to expect.

My heart is pounding, and I begin to sweat a little.

"Sandy Garcia!"

"BABE!" Cole shakes me, "that's you."

Followed by a round of applause and cheers, the room spun.

I made my way up to the stage as they announced Cole for Prom King as well. Hand in hand, we step into the spotlight of the well-lit stage.

Cheers and hollers filled the room, and it was never-ending. This felt surreal. They placed a gorgeous decorated crown on my trembling head, and a bouquet of roses was handed to be, and it was time for our first dance as Salem High's new Prom King and Queen.

"As we started our waltz, I felt safe in Cole's arms and wouldn't have wanted to share this with anyone else. Finishing up our dance, an unplanned announcement came through the speakers, and the music went off.

"We can't let our newest schoolmate go through prom without a proper welcome," the familiar voice nags across the mic.

Just as her irksome finished speaking, two cloaked, mystery people came to the stage and handed me a box.

"Open it," the crowd got quiet.

Opening the box to a dead rat!

"Is this supposed to be funny," Cole yells as I drop the box and run offstage and laughter fills the room.

"WELCOME TO SALEM HIGH SCHOOL," the voice over the intercom laughs.

"Sandy, wait!" Cole runs after me, "I'll find out who did this!"

"You know who did this, Cole," I get a bit aggravated.

"She needs to back off!"

"I know, I know," Cole grabs me and lifts my head and kisses me, "I know, don't pay them any mind, they are just jealous."

"Let's get you home," Cole grabs my hand, as we make our way on foot.

As we reached Gertrude's, Patrick was at the window.

"Can anyone be more dead, he looks like a statue from the wax museum," we both chuckled.

"I'm glad I met you, Sandy, you are one of the best things in my life, and I'm sorry if it feels like I am pushing you away but I....I just don't know what is going on I....I," I interrupt his stammering, with a kiss.

"It's fine, and I'm glad I met you too," I let him know I was listening.

Cole kisses me one last time, I think I'll get out of here.

"You're walking?" I question his sanity.

"Yeah, why not?" he pushes that he is ok.

"Let me take you home," I urge him to not walk in the night.

"I'm ok, I promise," he kisses me one last time before we slowly break our hands apart.

Closing the door

Gertrude is sitting in the living room with a book as usual

"I don't like that boy," I was surprised by that as she never seemed to have a problem before, "There is just something about him I don't like," as she gets up from her deeply imprinted couch to go watch Cole walk down the beat, dark path, that was covered in the unknown.

"Why is walking alone in the dark anyway….he isn't scared?" Gertrude questioning his authenticity.

"I guess not," I nonchalantly brush off Cole's walking habits.

"Well, aren't you going to tell me about prom?" Gertrude seemed semi-intrigued.

"I was, but then again the prom was hellish at the end, but my walk home with Cole made it better, I had forgotten all about it," I told Gertrude, I really just want to head to bed.

"Spit it out," Gertrude demands.

"Well, I was elected prom queen," I start the beginning of a disturbing story.

"WHAT! That is great."

"No, not so great," I go into details, "they handed me a shoebox… with a dead rat inside."

"What! Ugh fickles - they are no good, I told you that," Gertrude gloats at how right she was about the fickles.

"I know, I know," I roll my eyes.

"You, if I knew my magic well, I could have hexed them!" I got excited at the thought.

"We don't hex unless there is a danger and/or if we don't mind having, it reversed back to us," Gertrude explains to calm my cocky mind.

"I guess you are right, they are not that important," I convinced myself, "Now, I just want to go to bed, It has been a long night."

"Ok, my dear, we have lots to do in the morning, get rest," Gertrude promises me. Saying good night as I make my way through the dark hallways to my room. Closing my door and

plopping my exhausted body down on the bed, I sigh a sigh of

relief, as I smile thinking about Cole, I fall to sleep.

In the morning, the sounds of cabinets awoke me slamming, running downstairs, I trip and run into Patrick

"I am truly sorry, Ms. Garcia," Patrick moans.

"Why are you sorry, Patrick," I chuckle at his over-politeness as I make my way to the kitchen.

"Why, are the cabinets all slamming," I yell over there intrusive ratchet. Gertrude smiling, "You are in love......"

"What?" flipping around, "What do you mean."

"Well," Gertrude explains, "When a witch is in love, she can't control her powers for a few days, and since you are new at your powers, it might be a little longer."

"Really," I smile at the thought of loving Cole, and I can't break my grin.

"Get dressed my dear, we have work to do," Gertrude claps her hand and pushes me back upstairs.

Running up the stairs and catapulting myself in my room, grabbing whatever I come across on my floor, rushing to the back where Gertrude is waiting. My mind was stoked, today was a new day...literally a new day to begin the rest of my life - again.

"Now Sandy," Gertrude begins her lecture, "The key to a witches' magic …… is to believe, if your heart isn't in it, your magic fails and falls apart."

"Ok…ok," I urge Gertrude to get to the nitty-gritty.

"Let's begin," Gertrude says to me with such excitement, "Okay, my dear, we are going to start with something small."

As my eyes start bouncing around the area we were standing, a butterfly lands on a tall rosebush in the far corner of Gertrude's beautifully decorated masterpiece of a yard, Nicely designed to entertain only the bugs that live here.

"Okay, Sandy," Gertrude addressed me sharply, "Turn the butterfly a moth….."

"Okay," I say, overly confident, "This should be easy enough."

Overhearing Gertrude snickering under her breath, "Just believe what you want it to be, and it will be what you want."

Taking a deep breath, I point at the butterfly and say, "Okay butterfly turn into a moth," Nothing happens

Turning to Gertrude, "Well?"

"Sandy, my dear, us witches are natural poets," make up a spell in your head, say it out loud and mean it with passion." Gertrude proceeds to point at the butterfly and says, "Butterfly of color, turn into a moth of grey, please come again on another sunny day," the butterfly turns into a moth.

"My eyes grew more comprehensive, "Cooool, I think I can do that," I repeat Gertrude's poetic spell.

"Butterfly of color turn into a moth grey, please come again on another sunny day," the next thing I knew, the damn butterfly turned into a moth!

"OH yeah," as I jump up and down with excitement. Spinning around from thrill.

"Calm down, that was good, but let's go to something bigger," Gertrude points to a bluebird in the tree and says, "Change its color."

"To what?" I ask.

"To any color, you desire, my dear," Gertrude answers.

"Okay," I say as I rub my hands together, "Bluebird, Bluebird in the trees, I don't like you blue, so please turn green."

The bluebird shakes and explodes, "Oh my god, oh my god," I shriek and turn to look at Gertrude in horror, "What did I do!"

"It just takes some practice, my darling, you still have glitches in your blood, that will make your blood act up," Calming me down, "You just have to continue to practice, and all the glitches will get cleared out soon," Gertrude reassured me

"Now," Gertrude says, "We will practice on things other than nature."

"Like what?" I questioned in fear and wondered if I even wanted to know.

"On…. yourself," Gertrude hesitantly utters.

"Ummm, maybe that isn't such a good idea, I have only been at this for about a few hours, and I just exploded a bird!" I reminded Gertrude, in case she had forgotten.

"It is, okay, I am here to help you, my dear," Gertrude smiles at me with confidence, "Now, try to grow your fingernails…..and paint them.

"That's a lot to ask for," I sarcastically respond.

I look down at my hands and close my eyes, "Plain hands of mine, I need a fix, can you make them pretty and do it quickly."

I open my eyes to see 6 fingers on each hand, I freak out, "I said fix NOT six," I start shaking and jumping up and down, I trip and fall to the ground, "Gertrude!....HELP!!!"

Gertrude start laughs, "No worries my dear," she snickers, "The divine realm of magic, listen to me now she said she needs a fix, not six,"

My fingernails grew, and they get painted blue with glitter, "Oh nice," I smirked.

"Okay, Gerty, I've had enough magic for the day," I want to go inside now and rest, I've done more than enough.

"Oh my darling Sandy, you can never get enough of magic," as Gertrude dust off her hands and proceeds inside.

I follow without question

Gertrude pulls out a book

"More spells Gerty, no….I'm tired," I exclaim and refuse to move anymore, throwing my tantrum self in a chair.

"Relax, my dear, I am in charge of the annual Witches and Warlock balls tonight," She begins and I straighten up to listen in.

"There are 40 other witches and warlocks here in Salem, my dear," Gertrude professes, "I need to start the process and make sure we all have a ball!

"Go get cleaned up dear, they should be arriving any time soon," Gertrude insists.

I rush upstairs excited but nervous at the same time

Will they like a half-fickle?

Will I like them?

I dash upstairs to get ready. I'm sure to make some new friends.

Finishing up getting ready, I hear the doorbell ring. I run downstairs, and I am greeted by Becky Coft, a girl who speaks really fast, with long flowing burgundy colored hair, skinny and tall and Timmy Tolle, mid-height, dyed blonde locks, and brown eyes.

"Sandy, meet Becky and Timmy," Gertrude introduces me to them, their energy seems to be off the wall.

"H!!," Becky jumps in my arms, "Nice to meet you!"

"Timmy!" Timmy says as he holds his hand out.

"Have fun, guys," Gertrude leaves us to mingle.

"Want to go to my room?" I asked to get away from the adults

"Let's go!" Becky yells, "I'll race ya!"

Becky and Timmy take off up the stairs leaving me behind

"I like them," I say aloud to myself.

Reaching my room, the two already seemed to make themselves comfortable,

"So, Sandy," Becky jumps on my bed, "Who are you!?"

"Well, my name is Sandy, and I moved here a few months ago because my mom died…" I told them the whole story, my life, the deaths that plagued me.

"I'm only half fickle," as I end my story.

Becky chuckles, "You don't have to tell me," she says while laying back on my bed, "My dad told me already because your aunt already told him and he told me to be nice."

"I hope we can be friends for a long time," Becky shrieks to me.

"That would be nice," I got more comfortable, "I really haven't made many friends, even though I'm well-liked at school," I begin to explain my dilemma.

Timmy jumps, "WELL, I'm glad to see another young witch around here because they are not many of them in Salem anymore because it is hard to live a life if anyone finds out that you are one of the Ws (Witch, warlock, or wizard). This is why the Ws have to be close and stick with each other," Timmy nudges Becky, "Ain't that right, Becks!"

"That's right!" Becky smiles back.

"So, you two are home-schooled," I asked out of curiosity.

"YES! We must, we can't go to school with fickles; I'm surprised Gertrude allowed you too!" Timmy sounded amazed while swiping his bangs across his forehead with his flamboyant flair.

"Well, I'm half fickle who didn't know about the witch side of me until recently….It's what I am used to," I tried to explain to them.

Becky responds with a dumbfounded look, "Well duh Tim, she is only half," looking at me, "No offense but full witches wouldn't step foot in 'Fickle' school, it's too big of a risk to take," Becky continues, "And you of all, your powers might go haywire one day and destroy the school or something."

Becky and Timmy laugh, and I just sit there embarrassed.

"Sandy," I hear Gertrude call me from downstairs, "Excuse me, guys, I'll be right back."

Headed down the stairs, Gertrude meets me at the end.

"My darling, you have a phone call," Gertrude says with curiosity.

"A phone call?" I repeated, with enough more curiosity, as if I hadn't heard her the first time, "Is it, Cole?"

I don't know sweetie, I can't really understand them.

I hurried to the kitchen with curiosity running through her body. I rushed to the old, pure gold, English style phone that was correctly placed in Gertrude's kitchen.

"Hello?"

"Hi, Sandy," the other end responds.

My face goes pale, and my heart starts racing faster than the blood can catch up, and I knew that voice. It was an all too familiar voice, a voice that repeated in my head every day.....It was KY.

"KY?" I asked with nervousness.

"Yes - Sandy, how have you been?" he asked with all words of kindness.

"Fine.....good....um great, great," I responded, not sure of what to say. I couldn't believe it was him. I have been waiting for him to contact me for the longest, and just when I'm moving on, he calls me out of the blue.

"That's good, that's good," he responds, waiting to ask more questions. "Um, Sandy?"

"Yes," I responded, not sure of what his intentions were.

"I've been needing to speak with you and hear your voice," He begins, "I just wanted to let you know how sorry I am about the last time that we spoke," he continues. "I can't believe how much of a jerk I was, and I can't believe that I let you go without saying good-bye," he seems sincerely apologetic.

Finally, I rejoiced in my head at the sound of those words. I have been waiting for him to call and apologize. I felt terrible about leaving and not being able to say goodbye to him; even though I was mad, I still felt that I needed to say bye - to him.

"But why did it take you so long to call.....or even write to me," I insisted he give me a good explanation of his downfalls.

"I don't know Sandy, I... I guess, I feared rejection from you and I wasn't ready for that," he tried to convince me that everything he was saying was right, trying to convince my heart that he was authentically sorry.

"I haven't stopped loving you, Sandy, you know that, right?" he questioned me, "I think of you every day....I can't stop, it is like a terminal sickness, and it is tearing me up inside to know I can't see you as I want too. but I would like......"

"KY....," I had to interrupt him, afraid he might say more than he wanted to. Still, he needed to hear what I had to say, "I appreciate the apology, but you can't expect me to just drop everything and everyone and forgive what you had done, especially when I needed you the most." I got emotional.

"No, I wouldn't expect you too, I wanted to let you know how much your absence has made an effect on my life and I want you Sandy........and ONLY you," he confessed his love, "I tried ...I TRIED to forget about you, I tried to break myself away from everyone and anything that reminded me of -you," he pushed his story, "I'm going crazy Sandy, I don't know what is happening, but all I know is that - I NEED you....."

Those last two words sounded like nails on a chalkboard because Cole had been telling me the same thing, and now my emotions are going crazy. I feel like I can't control where my feelings are flying to. KY has been in my life a lot longer than Cole, but Cole has treated me like a princess since I met him, I had to second think everything.

"KY -," I hesitated, "I've missed you too, and I wish you would have told me this a long time ago because....but."

He interrupts me, with anger in his voice, "because you have someone new!" he explodes

"Yes, KY! But...., "I explained as if I owed him an explanation.

"No, there is no BUT Sandy.....don't try to keep me in the dark, tell me the truth and be honest," He raises his voice, "I love you, and I'm sure he will never love you as I do, we have known each other for a long time Sandy.......I mean, does he even know your favorite color.... your favorite food....movie, or even your family nickname?"

"Yes….yes he does KY," I start even though Cole didn't know all those things yet KY didn't need to know that, "And besides, even if he knew none of that and even if I still wanted you, you are not here KY," I cried my heart out, "And I couldn't put my heart through that," I got frustrated at KY. He thought just because he calls and apologizes, I would drop everything and everyone here to take him into my heart.

"But we could make it work Sandy, Just give us a try, please," he begs, I've never heard his voice break before, "I know we weren't able to make us work before, but maybe this could be a star," He pleads.

"KY," I stopped him, "I don't want us to lose what we have please……," I begged him with caution, the phone got unusually hot, and it was not in my imagination, it was like the tension coming from his body was radiating through the phone, it was weird.

"Are you okay, KY?" I had to ask him because I was sensing something…..something terrible.

"No…… no, Sandy, I'm not okay….I need you," His voice deepens.

His words seem to burn a hole through the phone and send shivers up my spine because those words hit me hard, like rocks against a glasshouse. I was afraid that he would not let me go smoothly. I had to try to calm him down in some way.

"Call me more KY…..send me letters…..let's start from there, okay?"

A long pause kept me anxiously waiting for an answer, it felt like a century. I wasn't sure how he would take this, but I wasn't just going to break up with Cole for KY who was miles and miles away even though; I didn't want to hurt either of them because they are both significant in my life, but I guess I just needed time.

"Ok, Sandy, but….."

And here comes the "but."

"I'd just wish you would tell me, *okay*, and leave it at that, I guess that is impossible."

My heart just started beating harder and faster at the thought of what else would come strolling out of his mouth.

"Only if I could at least come to visit you.....just once," he rolls the words from his tongue.

He said it, oh god.....he said what I was afraid of. I couldn't have him come out here if I saw him I think I would want to leave Cole for him and then KY would leave me alone with my emotions out of whack and Cole would never forgive me. I was unsure of what to say.

"We'll talk about this later, okay KY," I calm his mind, "We have guests over right now," I had to reassure him that I would think of everything, but I just needed some time to think about what I would say to him. I wanted to see him terribly wrong, but I didn't want the possibility of falling more in love with him and leaving Cole, who I was falling in love with broken-hearted.

"Okay," he responds reluctantly, "Call me back, Sandy, please...... I'll be waiting."

For some reason, every word he continued to say to me, my heart beat faster, I was sweaty, my stomach turned harder.

"Bye KY," I whispered to him as I hung up the phone slowly as I waited to hear if he had anything else left to say.

"Hey, stranger!" a voice behind me startles me. It was from Becky.

"You've been gone for a while, who was that?" she overly curiously asked.

I just let her know that it was someone who was once prominent in my life.

"A boy?" she asked with a smirk on her face, waiting for me to spill the juicy gossip that she knew I had secretly embedded in my head.

"Yes, but I don't want to talk about that right now," I argued with her, not wanting to start an entire detailed lecture about KY. I just wanted to have this day end already. I felt almost fatigued and didn't know why.

"Becky!" a deep voice shouted through the few people left in the living room.

"My dad," she shrugs under her breath, "Time to go," she informs me, "Hey, but don't be a stranger, I'm sure we will become best friends!"

I doubted without a second thought, I was a little closed-minded and wasn't looking to make any new "best friends," I had my girls back in Little falls, but I was willing to have a new friend in my life right now, I need to surround myself with some people.

"OK, sure," I gave her false hope in my response.

"Bye, Becky," I responded and hugged her and reassured her that we would hang out sometime. She hugs me with strength and leaves out the door with her father as they both seem to leave a lingering wave. As the rest of the party makes their departure to their homes. Gertrude tells her last goodbye to the ultimate guest, she closes the door and looks back at me with sadness and curiously all mixed into her eyes. She makes her way to the living room and pats the cushion to her left-side, as she encourages me to come to sit down and talk to her. She could feel my emotions, and they seem to be affecting her, I could tell she looked drained, and I felt the drainage that ran out of her body and appeared to flow back into mine.

"Talk to me, my dear Sandy," Gertrude appointed her ears to my words.

Should I tell her that my feelings for KY are starting to slowly appear, or does she already know and just wants me to confess my feelings of affection in a love triangle that I didn't know how to break?

"Gertrude," I hesitated to begin this conversation, not knowing how she would look at me, "I think I love two guys.....is that possible?"

She begins to laugh. Her laughter, in a way, made me feel relaxed and more comfortable.

"Of course, my dear," she responded without strain.

She stands up and heads towards the fireplace; she grabs a glass bowl that sits atop the black marble mantel. She reaches in and takes out what looked like purple ash.

"Come here, my darling," she urges me to come to her and sit by the fireplace.

"A witch being in love with two guys is actually very common," She reassures me, as she blows the dust into the fireplace. This seems to bring up a story of a woman being in love with two men,

"A witch lets off an erotic aroma that creates a divine sense of meaning and importance in a person's life. It is outside of anyone's control on how this happens," Gertrude continues, "But in the end, only one will win because once she falls for the two contenders, her body lets off a sense of panic and the two men usually end up in a battle over the witch."

Staring at Gertrude and trying to make sense of this all, "When a witch falls in love with two men, they become obsessed with her and there is no way to stop their emotions…..this is the only downfall."

My face fills with fear as I watch the movie play in the fire. I didn't want KY or Cole to fight or worse…..DIE because they have obsessively fallen in love with me, and in some way, their feelings were out of their hands. Now, I felt sad and feel like I have deceived them both, even though I did not know of this. During the fireplace movie, I feel a strong presence. My head spins around to the window, and I can feel that someone is outside.

"What wrong? Gertrude asks scarcely.

I approach the window and open the curtains up more than the silver that had been drawn to try to catch the peeping eyes that I had felt down my back, only to find the dust howling in the wind.

"Who is it, my dear?" Gertrude questioned my witchy senses.

"No one, I guess I was wrong," I responded, questioning my sanity. Gertrude reaches for the door with forcefulness and fearlessness

"Our senses are never wrong," Opening the front door, Gertrude takes a deep breath.

"I smell something...... a familiar smell, I can't quite put my nose on it, but they have been here before."

She continues to glance through the darkness, hoping to find the intruder running through the trees and down the dirt path that reaches Gertrude's house. She sees no one and closes the heavy brave, hard enough to shake the house.

"They are gone," She reassures me, "Shall we," Gertrude proceeds back to the center of the living.

I slowly head back to the living room but still curious about what just happened, I can't help but want to figure out who or what was here watching us and...why.

Chapter

11

COLE'S VIEW

"Can't believe what I just saw, are my eyes deceiving me," I continued huffing.

I had to run like the wind from that house. My dad will kill me! What have I done!

Rushing into the house, my dad is sitting in the living room reading the newspaper.

" What is wrong, Cole," my dad questions my fearful entrance through our thick wooden steel bar doors.

"Nothing!" I snapped with such anger, fear, and uncertainty, not realizing I yelled at my pops.

"Don't you get lippy with me young man!" my brazen dad approaching me with his chest bulked up, "Now, I asked you a question, you answer with respect–do we understand each other," my dad rightfully demanded.

"Yes, pops, I'm sorry it's just that...... I can't....I can't tell you."

With my dad glaring down his throat, now I know that was the wrong thing to say. My dad's persistent attitude will not stop until he gets an answer out of me.

"What is wrong, Cole?" my father now demanded, I needed to answer and answer quickly, his face was turning hot red.

I take a deep breath and swallow what I feel is my last breath.

"Well, I stopped by Sandy's house," I begin.

"And?" my dad insisted on a more precise response.

"She is a…," I reluctantly tell my dad.

"A what–you better get to talking, boy?" my dad gets closer and slams down the newspaper he had been holding tightly in his clutches.

"A…..witch," I blurted out of the mouth.

"WHAT!" my dad raises his deep voice with anger, "That girl was in my house!"

"I know pops, I know…. I didn't know, I swear," I nervously bent my head.

"You stop this, and you stop it now," my dad grew angrier, "If ever, I see her in or around you again! There will be hell to pay," my dad slammed his fist on the countertop crushing the beautiful Brazilian granite that was neatly taken care of.

I remained quiet.….I mean, what was I going to say….or do? Against my dad, disobey, run away?

"Do you understand me!?" my dad yells,

"Yeah.….yes….yes….," as I stand taller with my chest out.

As my dad returned to the living room clearly heated.….he sits down, he takes off his glasses, crushes them, and tosses them in the fire. Walking away, I was too intimidated to even turn around; I continued walking to my room, to be startled by a loud grunting roar.

This isn't good.

Chapter

12

Ogres

The next day at school, I see Cole, and I run to give him a hug and kiss him, but he gives me the cold shoulder, as his cousins look on. He holds his arms forward, so I could not get any closer. Growing angrier, I look at him, "What's wrong, Cole?"

He just looks away from me, like he never knew who I was.

"Cole," I grab his shoulder and turn him around.

"Sandy," he stops my words, "I need to talk to you, can you come over after school?"

"Yeah....sure," still trying to make sense of this all.

Standing a few feet behind him was June, just smirking and smiling and walks away. Does this have anything to do with June? My heart had felt hurt, and I didn't know what to think. Cole avoided me for the rest of the day at school.

Finally, after school, I arrived at Cole's house with nervousness and being more anxious than ever. I ring the doorbell and step back. Cole answers, and he lets me in a while, turning his back to me. Closing the door myself, I follow Cole's lead to the kitchen. He turns around with suck aggression, with his fist to mouth, "Is there anything that you would like to tell me?" he exclaims.

"Um, no…..why…..?" I asked Cole with agitation.

"No!" Cole replicates his harsh question.

"Nothing at all," he gets angrier and throws a glass across the room.

"Oh my god, Cole, what is your problem!" I questioned Cole's actions, perturbedly.

"Is June putting stuff in your head!" I eject my emotions at him,

"You know if you want to be…," Cole cuts me off.

"No, it is not her," he points in my face, "It is - YOU!"

"ME!" I question his motives on how he was speaking to me

"Stop - JUST stop," he gets more emotional, "Why didn't you tell me, Sandy…..Goddamn it!!" Cole paces across the room and talks to himself, punching holes in the wall and yelling. "I can't

believe this," tears form in his desolate eyes,

"I loved you, Sandy."

"Loved," I repeated, standing there with a shocked look on my

face when a loud thumping noise approaches….It was Mr. Creek,

Cole's dad.

"GET OUT OF HERE…. GET OUT OF MY HOUSE….,"

Mr. Creek exclaims, "IF YOU DON'T WANT TROUBLE,

GET….OUT! Mr. Creek approaches me with his bulky body,

getting bulkier by the minute.

Cole jumps in front of his dad, "Dad, stop!" he yells.

"I thought, I told you to get rid of this thing…...this….. (he looks

at me with disgust)….broom rider!" Mr. Creek blurts out in utter

madness.

Did he say that to me! What? How?

Surprised by his choice of words, I had to deny this, if anyone

knew, it would devastate us, "I don't know what you are talking

about," I cry out in denial

"Don't play innocent now, you rat stew, piece of nothing, worthless witch!!!" Mr. Creek explodes at me.

"POPS!" Cole jumps in to defend me, "She is the only thing that makes my heartbeat, my only way of being," Cole continues against his dad, "That is enough pops, I can't get rid of her okay.....I can't.....I LOVE her!!!!" Cole blurted out in extreme demolishment.

"What!!!" his dad explodes with anger.

Cole's cousins come charging in, arriving just in time to try to calm the situation. They all try to restrain Mr. Creek, they all fail, too much for them to handle.

I can't believe what I am seeing.....right before my eyes, a giant, green monster, with snarling teeth, muscles on top of muscles, veins popping out of every inch in his body, a bulging body out of nowhere.

There are other "things" out there like me...unnatural, different....

I'm lost in my train of thought, and I can't move, I can't breathe

My heart feels like it has a stop

"Sandy….," Cole grabs my attention, "Sandy….RUN," He

shakes me.

My body hesitated to make a sensitive move

"GET OUT...Sandy!" Cole screams holding back his dad

I dart out the door so fast…..do I dare look back?

I do

I lock eyes with…..IT.

Trying to grasp my reality around what I witnessed, he then pulls

a large horn out and blows, this god awful sound…..My ears ring,

and I turn to try to run…..I'm stuck….My body paralyzed

somehow. Fighting this urge, I break free from its binding sound,

cover my ears, and run…..this time, I don't look back!

Approaching the house in a panic, wondering how I go there so

fast, with sweat and tears running down my exasperated face. I

could barely fix myself to explain

"Gertrude," I scream, "….Gertrude!!!" I try to catch my breath.

Gertrude comes flying into the living room

"WHAT!.....WHAT!!!" she proclaims, caressing my face.

"They.....he," swallowing the saliva in my mouth, ".....them......

Cole," I break down. I can't breathe, I've lost all sense of the

world around me, what I knew or thought I knew.

"Monsters....horrible, horrible monsters.....," I scream to

Gertrude in exhausted liberation.

"WHAT!" Gertrude exclaims, "Orges,".....she says under her

breath with a snarl, "her eyes go bloodshot, and her body goes

stiff.

"What....Orges?" I ask, still in shock.

"Yes, filthy, dirty, maggot eating Orges.....I knew it....I knew

since the first time I smelled him," Gertrude snarled.

"I knew there was something I didn't like about him, and now I

know. Why didn't my senses go off for those THINGSSS," she

hisses as she takes off to 'the door.'

Smelling the air, her eyes widen, "They've gotten stronger, I

can't smell them like I used to."

"I'm so sorry my dear…. but I should have prepared you for this…..," Gertrude darts me a look

"For what?" I questioned with fear as my heartbeats.

"A battle…..," Gertrude says as she walks into her lair.

She tosses her "ingredients" into her cauldron, the room goes dark, the smokes rises, the shelves shake and floors quakes

"Now is the time to gather thy fellow witches. and warlocks, and wizards of all kinds to join in the fairground for a battle of all time."

The skylight above shoots open

Gertrude dips a wooden bowl into her cauldron and scoops up a portion of her potion and proceeds to the backyard.

I follow her with an overwhelming sense of curiosity.

As Gertrude stands in the yard about to pour her potion

"WAIT…..," Gertrude whips around with annoyance.

"We can't….. I can't do this Gerty," I feared the worst.

Her face filled with anger and hurt

"Will, Cole, get hurt?" I questioned out of love.

"Sometimes, my dear…," she begins, "Your heart has to get broken before it can heal, and I can't let us get ruined because of your puppy love."

"Bring thy fellow family to thy fairs grounds at once!"

Gertrude throws the potion in the air, which seems to form a tornado and dashes off into all different directions.

"Now…Sandy follows me," Gertrude exclaims.

I just watched the areas of the tornado fade away, only thinking of Cole. Why does this have to be? Why him? Why was I, a witch and him…. something bigger? My head was pounding, and I couldn't think straight.

"SANDRA," Gertrude yells once more, "inside, NOW!"

We return to Gertrude's secret room. She opens a closet and throws me what looked like a tarnished, medieval blanket, "I was going to wait to show you how to use this, but there is no time…..it's your cloak," she smiles but with fear in her eyes. She then turns and digs through more stuff and hands me a broom. As she holds it across her palms and looks to the sky.

"Now the time has come to pass you down, you go with Sandy and make her proud."

Gertrude stands the broom up, and it almost jumps to my hand with extreme force

"I can't do this!" I yell at Gertrude and run out the door. I need to clear my head, as I proceed down our graveled pathway hidden by hoards of trees, I am yanked upwards with a vengeance. It was Gertrude on her broom, carrying me away, whether or not I wanted to. "Whether or not you like it, we are in this to the end," She demands my attention, "You have to fight Sandy, this is a gift, a gift to be a part of the Galva family." Gertrude exclaims, "This is what we do, we protect our family, our life - our magic."

"Do you understand me!" She snaps once again.

"Yes, yes, I do, but I don't think I can," I tell Gerty, "I'm not ready."

"You'll be fine," She reassures me while grabbing my face.

Chapter

13

FIGHT OR FLIGHT

We arrive at the fairgrounds, all waiting for us are 35 more witches, warlocks, and wizards. I see Becky, "Becky!" I call out!

We embrace each other for what seems to be a lasting one.

"I hope you are ready, Sandy," Becky says.

"I'm not Becky, I'm not…," I begin my pathetic sob story.

Suddenly the ground starts shaking, and I stumble along with Becky as I clenched her hand

"It's time," she smiles and drags me along beside her.

Slowly turning my head to the sound of howling, snarling, growls in the far distance, not knowing what to make of this. I wasn't ready; I can't….

Gertrude shouts out without fear, "Family, get ready!"

My head spins

In the distance, substantial monstrous ogres approached. Snarling sharp teeth, massive veins, popping muscles approaching fast with a constant force.

"I can't run now," I say to myself.

All of a sudden, four stumpy ogres shoot from the ground like fireworks on the 4th of July, causing the ground to crack and crumble beneath everyone. Once, the dust cleared standing there behind those four stood, six more who appeared….bulkier, more prominent, more substantial….. and Cole included. My heart sank, I knew this day would not end well. I knew there was nothing I could do to stop this or reverse what was already happening. All I could do was wish that everything was normal…..I don't want this. We were on opposite sides of enemy lines and had to defend our families and push the love we had for one another aside. Cole and I lock eyes, and my heart was crushed.

"ATTACK!" a voice screams in the far. As rock fireballs are being slung towards us in a catapult!

Hitting Becky and her mom

"Becky," I scream!

"Kill it!" Becky's father exclaims as he rises into the air with such ferocity, casting a stream of lightning, electrocuting the ogre, sending him flying backward like a bowling ball, hitting the ones standing behind him like the pins in a lane.

This starts the beginning of a colossal battle. "Mr. Creek," they scream. "Destroy them all!"

"All…," Gertrude yells, "take to the sky!"

All the enchanters, both big and small, old and young; rise up to prepare for yet another attack, this one was sure to end all attacks. I couldn't believe what was happening, I wanted none of this to happen. I feel like I'm in a daze, and there is no way out. I am cursed, and there is no way of getting rid of this. Everything's in slow motion, I glimpse every piece of dirt that flies past me, every action around me seems to slow down, just enough for me to breathe.

I look down at my hands, they're sparking, they've never done this, "Oh no no no, nothing new please, I tell myself," I look to Gertrude for guidance, only she's not paying attention.

"Superior attack!" Gertrude shrieks for obedience.

All the witches and warlocks take off in flight into the air, into the stormy clouded grey abyss but I can't follow, I wasn't prepared, I'm not ready,

The ogres find this is the time to attack the weakest one–me.

"POPS…. stop!" Cole yells at his father over the sounds of the battle between the two sides.

"You want to defend them!" He gets in Cole's face, "HER!" Cole's dad pushes him with such force that cole loses his balance and falls.

"Enough," His voice trembles as he gets up and gets back in his dad's face

"I love her!" Cole screams, "I can't watch you do this."

"Then you will die as well," his cousin proclaims, from behind. With disbelief running through Cole's mind, and sadness that his own flesh and blood would disown and wish death upon him because he can't control his feelings.

"Do you see what she has done to you, Cole!" His dad approaches Cole's face, "ARE YOU STUPID SON!" he screams at Cole, "It is in a witches nature to trap your heart–don't be DUMB!" he dad snaps with tears forming in his rock hard eyes.

"Now," Mr. Creek turns towards Sandy and screams for the bow and arrow ogre to strike.

"Kill her!" As Mr. Creek points the bow and arrow at Sandy's heart.

"Dad….NO!" as Cole gets up and strikes his dad with his fist, who seems to have his feet glued to the ground.

"Defend her again….," Mr. Creek scolds Cole with cold, hard eyes, "You are out of this family!".

Cole stares at Sandy, pushes past his dad, and runs towards her trying to catch her before the bow and arrow does.

"Sandy, move!!!" Cole screams, but I am unable to make out his words, I'm stuck, frozen at the moment.

Mr. Creek, in disbelief, calls out, "COLE!!!!"

I see Cole running towards me but still unable to move. What is he doing? What's going on?

I look up from the trance and see an arrow that was headed my way, unable to defend it.

"SANDY NO," Cole screams in pure terror.

Cole jumps in the way of the arrow! In extreme astonishment and fear, Cole gets hit!

"COLE NOOOO," I cry out in complete heartache.

As Cole gets turned back into his natural form, I drop to my knees.

"COLE!" tears come to my eyes

I couldn't believe what I just saw. I felt my heart drop into my stomach. My heart crushed, my soul torn from my body. Cole lands on the ground with an arrow through his shoulder passed out on the ground at my feet. Did I cause this? All I can do is put the blame on myself.

"Please wake up Cole," I caress his beautiful face, "Please.....," I plead, "I love you," as a tear falls on his face.

"HE saved her!" All Mr. Creek saw was red, "I will kill her myself!"

Mr. Creek charges with a bludgeon club towards me as I look up.
At that moment, the ground trembles, and I could only wonder
what is next in this cruel battle to appear. I look up to find him
heading my way without a care in the world.

I kiss my hand and rub Cole's forehead as I stand up.

I threw my hands up, hoping to let out a stream of lightning.......
nothing.

"How do these work," I yell at myself, frustrated at my
half-fickleness that has cursed me.

Nothing is happening, what do I do! What do I do! As Mr. Creek
approaches me, all I can do is prepare myself for the worst! I
stand tall and close my eyes, When out of nowhere, I hear a
gruesome screech that scares me more than the ogre charging at
me. I dip my head in my hands as if that would help. Then,
calmly I look up with caution.

"What in the....!" I look on in fearful amazement, this day keeps
getting weirder and weirder

That can't be

A dragon.....

Am I dreaming?

A giant dragon flew through the sky, knocking the clouds apart, causing a dust storm and landing on the ground in front of me with such force that it created a crater, followed by a massive howling screeched that made everyone cover their ears in pure agony.

It then let out its massive screech once more time toward the Orges, causing them to halt in their tracks fearing the worst, it shoots a mammoth stream of fire at the ogres, burning, scaring them to stand down

"CHARGE!" Mr. Creek demands, to the hesitated group of Ogres.

They charge the massive creature with no advantage. Finally, scaring the ogres off back to their rightful place, defeat filled the surrounding air.

At this moment, I screamed for Gertrude only to notice her in the sky with the rest watching the Orges take off in fright and keeping their 3rd eye on this new encounter.

I scream once more, "GERTRUDE!"

Her eyes dart in my direction.

"SANDY!" she shrieks, "Catch!"

She throws me my broom that had been attached to her. It reaches me in velocity-time and connects to my hand like a fitted leather glove. Now, only to figure out how to ride it. My first attempt failed, it seems to have run out of gas, as I am about 50 feet in the air. Falling back to the ground but with my nerves still tight as I look back at the dragon who seems to catch my eyes.

"Why did you look it in the eyes, Sandy," I question myself in my confusioned mind, boggled by my stupidity.

I hop on my broom, "Let's try this again."

I start a mini-run and begin to take off

"COMMAND IT!" Gertrude screams.

"Faster!" I commanded.

I take off, It's up, I'm going... I got it.....now... where is this beast?

I look behind me.......nothing....I smirked a bit, only to feel a gust of wind coming from above. I look up and then forward to see IT, it lands on the ground in front of me with a perfect glide. I get rightfully startled, and I tumble off my broom at the site of the dragon feet, hitting my head on a rock. I got knocked unconscious, My entire life flashed before my eyes. I saw my mom, Jayco, and dad. Was this it, was I dead.......

I come in and out of consciousness,

I feel overpowered, but with a sense of calmness, I wasn't afraid.

But who was carrying me.....

As I slowly open my eyes, my breath gets taken away

"Everything is okay, Sandy, I'm here....," a familiar voice tells me. "I'm here now."

I can't believe it.....

"KY……"